Little Sanctuary

RANDY BOYAGODA

Little Sanctuary

TRADEWIND BOOKS
Vancouver • London

For Anna, and for Mira, Olive, Ever and Imogen:
My great sanctuary—RB

The children have no time to be children . . .

Franz Kafka

1

HOW DO YOU FIND SWEET SYRUP at the end of the world?

There were seven dishes on the table. This was the family's last meal before they left home. The children were dressed as if for school. They wore white shirts, navy shorts, navy socks and black shoes.

The seven dishes:

For Sabel, a plate of melon slices.

A towel of warm bread for her sister Reya.

A foiled bit of chocolate for her sister Theri.

A bowl of plain cold rice for her sister Verlane.

A cup of pitted cherries for her brother S'Jin.

A cup of black olives for Appa.

A bowl of sour yoghurt for Amma.

A thimble of sweet syrup for Amma.

They held hands.

No one said anything after that.

Someone has to say something, thought Sabel. *Otherwise it will be just another day.*

Each had their favourite food, some of it miraculously found, and the children were wearing their school uniforms for the first time in a long while. But still, just another meal. They would eat, as usual, while listening for the sound of planes, of trucks, of when it was time to go back down into the cellar and wait in the dark with candles until the sounds stopped. Then see if there was still an upstairs.

But this time, this meal, they were listening for a new sound too. Another terrible sound.

No, not terrible. Apparently.

Hopeful.

Apparently.

"Remember, children, what we are doing, where we are going . . ." Appa said.

". . . is because we are hopeful" Amma finished the sentence.

Amma and Appa keep saying this, Sabel thought, *as if to believe it themselves.*

They ate in the big cold kitchen where they also slept these days, the one room of their house that still felt like a room of their house. Along its western side were smashed-in walls, a caved-in roof, and debris from the bomb that had dropped nearest to them.

So far.

The night the bomb dropped, Sabel felt a strange cold wind come down the stairs. After climbing out of the cellar, Appa and Amma argued about whether the house was a target.

They lived so far from the city. There were no other houses near them.

Be hopeful, but be careful when you trust.

"Touch only those you are committed to for the rest of your lives," Amma had told them.

"Maybe it was meant for the capital," said Appa. "Maybe it was an accident."

"How could this be an accident?" Amma exclaimed.

"It was an accident. It had to be an accident."

"Why *had to be*?"

"They've already killed the president. Why kill his doctors now?"

"Can someone bigger than me go close the door upstairs?" asked Theri. "The wind makes me . . ."

"Scared!" teased Verlane.

"No!"

"Verlane, go upstairs and close the door," said Sabel.

"No. I'm scared," said Verlane.

"Ha!" said Theri.

Sabel went upstairs and closed the door.

Someone, say something, thought Sabel, looking at everyone motionless and staring at the favourite dishes.

But no one spoke after the prayer. No one was eating, either. Sabel knew why. Starting meant they would have to finish, and after clearing the table, it would be time to leave home.

So instead, they looked at one another. Everyone's hands kept going up to scratch behind their ears, to rub the backs of their necks.

Late afternoon, the day before, Amma and Appa had called Sabel to come behind the house, below the ash-covered trellis wrapped in dead vines. Birds were still singing in the far field. Beyond that, on a clear day, you could see the capital. Buildings like white, silver and black streaks against the sky. Mostly black by now. But from here, the city looked peaceful.

Amma turned the metal garden chair in the other direction, toward the sloped side of the gully where the river still ran.

Amma made Sabel sit in the chair, wrapped a towel around her shoulders and cut her hair very short, sporting-day short. Then she called Sabel's younger sisters—fourteen, twelve, ten—and her eight-year-old brother. After cutting everyone's hair—*Why, Amma?—Sit still!*—Amma sat down and called Appa over. Everyone watched and giggled while Appa cut Amma's hair, but when Amma saw herself in the mirror in the kitchen, she cut it again.

"I thought you had the hands of a surgeon?" Sabel teased.

"I used to," Appa replied.

"We all look like soldier boys now," said Sabel.

"Soldier boy!" said Verlane. "Send him your hair in the mail."

"Amma!" said Sabel, wincing.

"What mail? Who?" asked Appa.

"She likes him! She likes him!" sang Verlane.

"Sabel, did you give someone our address?" Appa demanded. "A soldier?"

"Sabel!" said Amma.

"Amma!" Sabel cried.

◆ ◆ ◆

Amma picked up the thimble of sweet syrup. She marvelled at it. She looked at Appa, as if to say: *Melons and fresh bread, fine; even chocolate is probably hiding somewhere close.*

"How on earth did you find sweet syrup at the end of the world?" Amma asked him.

He looked back. "I found it for you."

Amma smiled, Appa smiled back, and then she poured it, very slowly, into the bowl of yoghurt.

With both hands, Amma picked up the bowl, tilting it. The dark syrup made circle after circle in the yellow-white yoghurt. The circles began to fall into one another and onto her fingers holding the bowl at the rim. The children watched in silence, then cheered.

They all began eating like never before, offering their treats back and forth and accepting and laughing and talking about what next.

What next?

They finished and got up to take away the dishes.

"Leave them," said Appa. "Never mind the cleanup."

"Never mind? Never mind the cleanup?" said Sabel. "Appa? Really?"

"Sit down. All of you, sit down. There is something we have to say. You will understand when you understand," said Amma. "From now on, your brother is your sister."

"I don't have a brother. Or, wait, is Amma having a baby?" asked S'Jin.

"No, S'Jin, you have sisters," said Appa.

"I want a brother. I don't even get to play with Tric anymore."

"Listen, S'Jin, from now until I tell you otherwise, you are their sister."

"Appa?" said Sabel. "Amma?"

"Sabel, you are the oldest," said Amma. "You have to help them understand."

Sabel nodded. She wanted to say: *Yes, I am the oldest. I will. But can you help me understand, first?*

"I can help too, Amma," said Reya, the second oldest.

"Yes, you too, Reya. Both of you."

"Amma—"

"Sabel! You have to!"

"No, Amma, listen," said Sabel. "Everyone, listen. Listen!"

A black bus with tinted windows pulled up in front of the house, red dust sprayed along its sides. While the family watched from the front walk, two men stepped out. They were dressed in black, with black-strapped visors, black sunglasses and short thick beards like smudges of black paint. Their only colour was the red dust on their black boots. One had a white scar that ran from cheek to cheek and stood out against his beard like tracer fire. They didn't have guns, at least not showing.

"Time to go," the scarred one said.

The scarless man took their bags—little sacks that each had promised they would be able to carry by themselves.

"Girls, you go first," said Appa.

No one moved.

"Girls, get on the bus!" said Amma. "Sabel! Reya! Take your sisters and get on."

No one moved.

"Okay, Amma," said S'Jin. "I'll go first."

S'Jin stepped into the bus. He had to use his hands to climb the stairs. He stood at the front, beside the driver, who looked the same as the other men. The driver stared ahead, tapping the steering wheel. S'Jin clapped the dust from his hands and waved to someone sitting at the back.

Through dark windows, Sabel watched the shaded shape of him walk the length of the bus.

Appa suddenly let out the worst noise. It was a screaming, raging, crying, sobbing sound, all of it choked, bubbling up in his throat, seeping through clenched teeth. He turned away from them. He turned back and held up his hands, palms facing them, fingers spread out, like he was surrendering. He kept pressing his shaking hands into the empty air. Like he was hitting against an invisible wall, trapped inside.

Not Amma, Sabel noticed. Amma had steady hands. She took each of Sabel's sisters by the shoulders and guided them into the bus. Her hands were sticky. The syrup. The two men climbed in, the door closed and they drove away, Amma and Appa disappearing in the dust.

Sabel didn't cry. She didn't ask any questions, at least not aloud. Surrounded by her sisters, all sobbing and pleading, she looked out the window, going over their final days at home, realizing, now, what Amma and Appa had been doing and planning. The whole time they said they were going away together, as a family, but instead planned to send just the children away.

Amma and Appa, figures in the back window, getting smaller and smaller in the red dust of the world.

S'Jin didn't cry either. His friend Tric was on the bus when it came for them. They hadn't seen each other in months. One row back from the sisters, the boys talked and talked—about recently seen animals, dead and alive; about the best and worst places they'd slept since the world had started to fall down; and about their marble collections. Meanwhile, the black bus sped past abandoned houses, burned-out cars, skinny cows, masked and bandaged people running toward the road at the sight of their bus, and others running from the road when they sped by. Old blockades and checkpoints lay on the side of the road, a collection of twisted metal. Gone were the men who once stood in front of them and asked questions.

"Why are your sisters crying?" Sabel heard Tric ask S'Jin.

"Ask them yourself. Sabel, my haircut is making me feel cold."

They took the main road toward the capital until it ended in a T. The bus turned right. This was also new to the children. When they used to travel between the city and their house in the country, they had always turned left.

Where were they going?

"There's a man on the bridge," the driver said to the other men.

Up ahead, an old man in a fine black suit stood in the middle of the bridge, facing the bus.

"That's the judge," whispered Verlane. "The twins are with him!"

"Ask the judge! Ask him when Amma and Appa are coming!" said Theri. "He's the judge! He'll know!"

Sabel already knew Amma and Appa weren't coming. When they had all lived in the city, before the store windows were smashed and pictures of the president torn down, the judge would come to their house some nights and sip from small cups with Appa on the veranda. They probably talked about what was happening, what was next.

The judge had two granddaughters, twin girls who played with Reya sometimes. They were standing on the side of the bridge with their bags.

"What do I do?" the driver called back.

"Drive!" said the scarred man.

He drove on. The judge didn't move. The bus reached the bridge, its tires rumbling on the steel. The old man stood his ground. The children were screaming.

Sabel jumped out of her seat, ran to the back of the bus and pulled S'Jin and Tric into her, covering their eyes. Reya did the same with Verlane and Theri.

"Okay, okay, stop. Stop!" shouted the unscarred man.

The bus shuddered and stopped in front of the judge. Sabel watched the two men get out. One stayed by the door and the other went to speak with the judge, keeping his distance. The judge pointed to his grandchildren and brought his hands together. A prayer? A request? Both? The twins looked tired and embarrassed.

"How did he know we were coming? That's not supposed to happen," the driver said to the unscarred man standing by the open door.

"He must have applied for his kids but didn't have enough money."

"We need to move. We can't be stopped like this, on a *bridge*," said the driver, leaning over to look up at the sky.

"Okay," said the unscarred man.

Through the bus window, Sabel saw him pull a pair of blue rubber gloves over his black gloves, walk over to the scarred man and say something into his ear. The scarred man didn't bother with extra gloves. Taking one arm each, they dragged the judge to the side of the road. The judge turned toward the children, begging and gesturing at them. The unscarred man shoved him in the chest with an open hand and the judge fell backward. He looked about to get up when the unscarred man took a step forward. The judge stayed down. The twins cried out and ran over to him. Sabel and the others watched as the unscarred man peeled off his blue gloves and dropped them on the bridge.

As they drove on, Sabel remembered coming to this place once before. She had been very little, and Amma brought her along while delivering metal boxes to another doctor. It was a different world here, even though it was so close to the city they had always known, the capital—always clean and new and wide open, its gleaming fountains and bright, clipped greens. Until it was charred and empty. *How long*, Sabel wondered, *until it is nothing at all?*

This place was called the Old City—it had always been as Sabel was seeing it now. There were no walkways or roads, just winding narrow lanes of pounded brick. The buildings were small and made of painted stone. In front of the buildings were barrels and vendors' stands and carts blocked on either side of each dusty wheel. The barrels, stands and carts were mostly empty. The market men and women, wearing chains and charms from unknown times and places, stood and sat beside their few faded wares. At their feet stretched dogs and cats, idle and taut as forgotten bows and arrows. The people were very old, all of them, their faces like shrivelled grape skins. They watched the bus as it drove past.

There were dwellings everywhere, along boulevards lined by leafless trees, the gnarled, reaching branches of which looked like the fingers of giant old men arguing with the sky. People lived on top of the buildings—and beside them and behind them—buildings made of old wood and scrap metal, their roofs waterproofed by the orange-and-blue tarps. The tarps rolled like waves in a storm.

No one follows rules here, Sabel thought.

People were everywhere, close together, many barefaced in spite of the illness. They moved in the same direction as the bus: toward the harbour, to boats waiting in the harbour. For a moment, Sabel looked for Marygirl among the people. Marygirl, who had been their servant until one day she was gone. But even if she were there, was one of them, what did it matter? Sabel at least knew this much by now—these men who would have run over a judge weren't going to stop the bus to let in an old servant woman.

Sabel looked away from the crowds. She edged her way up the aisle to the front of the bus, where the two men sat in the first seats behind the driver. They were looking straight ahead, ignoring the stares of all the people.

"Can you tell me where we are going?" Sabel asked.

"You will find out on the boat," one of them said.

"What boat?"

"Go sit down," said the other man.

"Sabel!" Theri, coming up behind her, said. "Sabel, give them this."

Sabel turned. "Go back to your seat, Theri. Stay with Reya until I come back."

"No. Just give them this," Theri insisted, holding out her hand. On her palm was the foiled bit of chocolate. "Give them this to tell us when Amma and Appa are coming."

"Sit down," said the scarred man. "We are almost there."

Sabel turned and put her hands on Theri's shoulders, but Theri slipped down and squeezed past her. "Here! Men! You can have this, all of it. Tell us when our Amma and Appa are coming."

The men didn't look at her. The bus went over a bump. The foiled chocolate fell under a seat. Sabel picked it up and grabbed Theri and led her to the back of the bus and made her sit beside Reya.

"What did they say?" Reya asked.

"That we'll find out everything on the boat."

"We're going on a boat?" S'Jin asked.

"Yes," said Sabel, trying to sound like she'd always known this was the plan.

"We had a boat," said Tric. "My Appa once caught a shark and I helped reel it in."

"For Reya's birthday, we swam with dolphins," said S'Jin.

"Shark," countered Tric.

S'Jin slumped down in his seat, defeated for this round between them.

"You should eat your chocolate before it falls in the water," Verlane told Theri.

Instead, Theri put the chocolate back in the little secret pocket sewn into her bag. She went to the back of the bus and looked out the window.

"Maybe Amma and Appa are following," she said.

"Maybe there's a second bus for the Ammas and Appas," said Theri. She had been looking back the whole time they were driving.

There wasn't a second bus behind them.

There's never going to be a second bus, Sabel thought.

"What are you going to tell them when Amma and Appa don't come?" Reya whispered to Sabel. "When they put us on the boat and Amma and Appa don't come?"

"I will tell them something," said Sabel.

"Why did they keep saying we had to be hopeful? How is this hopeful?"

"I'll tell them something," said Sabel.

"Sabel, tell *me* something. Tell me what's happening. I'm next oldest. Tell me."

But what could Sabel tell anyone . . . even tell herself?

The bus stopped. Ahead were the harbour docks and, off to the side, the shallows, where the tops of old and broken pier pillars stuck out like headstones. At the docks, people were climbing onto vessels of all sizes. More of the same people making their way to the ships were now in front of the bus and all around it. Everyone seemed to be moving, but no one was gaining ground. Sabel and the other children were the only ones riding in a vehicle.

The driver honked. No one paid any attention. He honked again and again, then opened the door, and the men sitting behind him leaned out and shouted at the people to move out of the way, but no one paid any attention. The driver honked. The men yelled. The crowd only gave way when four young men with big grey rifles walked up to the bus. One of the many militias. They wore jeans and sneakers and jackets over white T-shirts. Apart from the guns, they looked like they were on their way to a soccer game at the presidential stadium.

Before the stadium became the new prison.

"Checkpoint checkpoint checkpoint," S'Jin sang. Tric joined in for a verse before Sabel gave them a look. The other children had already ducked into their seats and were peeking out the windows. They watched the two men on the bus speak with the young men through the open door. There was a lot of pointing at the docks.

To Sabel, the two men on the bus were no longer mysterious and terrible monsters who had taken them away from their parents a couple of hours before. Now they were the less mysterious and less terrible men who would protect them from these more mysterious and more terrible men holding big long guns.

Did the two men from the vehicle have guns? Where were they? Shouldn't they get them out?

One of the men turned back into the bus and took something out of a bag under his seat. It wasn't a gun. It was a bundle of coloured papers that he counted out, putting most of it back into the bag. He stepped off the bus and gave the papers to one of the young men.

"Ghee," said Verlane.

After Amma and Appa had burned all their old money—the kind with the president's face on it that used to get them wherever they wanted to go—they had to use this new money, the kind everyone now called ghee. They used ghee to bribe the young men with guns who set up blockades everywhere. If you didn't have enough ghee to give, the men would start shouting, fingers on triggers, and then others would appear from bushes, bats and knives ready. Who were all these young men with guns and bats and knives? Where had they come from? How were there so many, and so angry, all of them? Where were they before the president had been taken away and the whole world felt like it was falling down?

Sabel had heard these questions being asked again and again while helping Amma in the kitchen the day the president's cooks, lawyers, zookeeper and his children visited them at their country house after his death. But no one had answers. Knowing that Sabel wanted to understand the circumstances, Amma had asked each of the adults gathered in the kitchen if they knew what happened to Marygirl, the family servant. No one knew. It was the kind of question they were all learning not to ask.

What other questions were there? What answers? Sabel had stayed with the adults in the kitchen while the rest of the children played under the trellis behind the house. Eventually the kitchen became quiet. She could tell she was not wanted there, inside, listening to adults asking questions no one could answer. Amma should have told the other adults that even if Sabel was only sixteen, she was old enough to stay with them. But Amma didn't tell them that. Instead Amma told Sabel to "Go watch the others and make sure they don't go down to the gully."

As in, the other children.

Outside, they had already run out of games and stories, and Sabel's sisters and little brother had finally accepted that the zookeeper's children weren't going to tell them what had happened to all the animals. And so, giving up on zoo news, they turned their energies to singing their newest song.

Checkpoint checkpoint checkpoint.

While the children sang, Sabel looked back to the kitchen, wondering what kinds of other questions she wasn't allowed to hear.

One of them, posed to Amma and Appa, must have been, *Are you going to send your children away?*

This was their plan.

They had told the others they didn't have a plan.

Which was part of the plan.

In a world falling down, Sabel sensed that old friends could become new rivals.

The bus began to move, very slowly, with two militia men out in front, clearing the way to the harbour.

"Which one is our boat, Sabel?" Theri asked. "I don't like the big ones. They look like shark heads."

"No they don't," said Verlane.

"She's right," said Tric.

"Which one of us is right?"

Tric just nodded wisely.

"Then what do they look like, Verlane?" asked Theri.

"Floating morgues."

"Verlane!" Reya hissed. "How do you even know that word?"

Sabel wasn't the only who had been listening to the adults.

"Everyone, stop!" Sabel cried.

The bus stopped.

For a moment, Sabel was amazed and reassured that she suddenly had such command over the situation. But these feelings went away after the militia men outside turned from the bus and walked away.

Where are they going? Sabel thought as the crowd filled in the space around the bus. The people looked the same as the ones they had seen in the Old City. Tattered, bundled, tired, limping to the harbour, wearing and carrying and pushing and pulling everything they had left. Children sat on shoulders, and babies were wrapped and strapped to chests and backs. It was an inky, cloudy day, but everyone looked like they were squinting against the sun.

"Someone else needs their help," said Reya. "Look over there."

The other children followed her pointing hand, as did the driver and the two men sitting up front. Outside, the militia men were walking toward a tighter crowd that had formed within the crowd. Someone in the middle was being held.

The militia men reached the person at the centre of the throng. A young man being jostled, no, beaten. They handed out a few coins and dispersed the crowd. The young man stood up and faced the militia.

Sabel moved toward the front of the bus to listen to the men speaking to each other.

"They're trying to recruit him," the driver explained. "He will accept their recruitment offer. If he refuses, he'll be made to accept it."

Outside, the young man coughed and spat at the militia men. They lowered their visors. Truncheons appeared.

"Children, go to the other side of the bus. Now!" shouted the driver, looking in the rearview mirror, and when they didn't move right away, he turned around in his seat and began to stand.

They moved over.

"Is that why S'Jin is now our sister?" Reya asked Sabel. "Would they take little boys and make them fight too?"

"It depends how long this goes on."

"What goes on, Sabel? The war or the sickness?"

Sabel just nodded. Reya went back a few rows to speak with Tric and S'Jin. To make sure they understood why S'Jin had to be known as their sister for now. The driver started honking again. A new set of militia men walked up to the bus, insisting they knew nothing of the earlier arrangement. More money came out of the black bag.

"Gee," said Theri.

"It's *ghee*," shot Verlane.

Theri rolled her eyes.

Sabel didn't know if she should be grateful for her siblings' bickering. Their old lives had come to an end weeks ago, and their new lives had come to an end hours ago—but they were still just children.

How much longer can they stay the same? she wondered. *Why didn't Amma and Appa tell me their plan? Only me, at least. I would have understood. I would have kept the secret. I kept other secrets for them, about them.*

Sabel had kept secret from her siblings what she knew about the sickness. Amma had told her it was a hungry kind of sickness, and it would eat up your insides the way snakes could eat up the inside of birds' eggs: you couldn't tell what had happened until suddenly the shell collapsed into itself.

"We should have stayed together as a family," Reya said.

"Amma and Appa should have been allowed to join us," Theri said.

"I could have kept watch at night," said S'Jin.

"What about everyone left behind?" Verlane asked.

Sabel shuddered, shutting the thought away in her head like an upstairs room. She didn't want to know. She would ignore this wind, just as she had ignored the wind that had come through their country house after the bomb fell.

The bus began moving again, and Sabel could see the new pair of militia men clearing a path to the docks. The bus reached the foaming dark-blue water, where the militia men turned, waved at the driver and walked away. The crowd here was parting on its own, moving toward either the big ships by the docks or the yellow rafts floating in the shallows along the shore. The bus drove ahead slowly, as if it were going straight into the water. A man on the dock motioned them forward. He was standing beside a control panel. The bus dipped and rocked from side to side. They were parked on a floating platform.

"We're here," said the driver, turning off the engine.

"Where?" asked Theri. No one answered.

The man from the dock walked around the bus, bending down here and there. Sabel watched his progress from her window.

"He's probably checking for bombs," said Tric.

"We're not a bomb," said S'Jin.

"How does he know?" said Tric. "How do you?"

"Is he going to give us the sickness test?" asked Theri.

"We're not sick!" said S'Jin. "We have the haircuts that show we don't have the sickness!"

The bus swayed on the platform. The children were quiet. Sabel stood up and marched to the front of the bus.

"Where are we going?" she asked.

"Go sit with your sisters," said the scarred man.

"No," Sabel said. "You know where you're taking us. Our parents have given you money to take us somewhere, and you are going to tell me, now, where we're going."

She pressed her hands into the back of the seat so the men wouldn't see them shaking. The men stared at her. The scarred one had a funny smile. The unscarred one looked irritated.

"Answer me, now," said Sabel. "Answer me . . ."

A roaring sound interrupted her and the bus began to shake,

shifting on the bucking platform. The children screamed and ducked down. From a half crouch, Sabel could see that the two men hadn't even flinched. She stood up and looked out the back window. The crowd was still moving toward the ships. A few were watching their bus on its platform, which was now slowly motoring out over the breaking waves. A couple of boys threw rocks at them, which fell well short and disappeared into the dark water.

The floating platform moored against the side of a big ship, scratched in two long lines up the hull, and the children lined up in the aisle of the bus.

This is like those field trips we used to take to an ancient ruin or a patriotic museum, Sabel thought.

The scarred man got out and went around to get their bags. The unscarred man motioned for everyone to come forward. They stepped down from the bus onto the platform, steadying themselves against the roll of the waves. From a distance, Sabel could still see the man at the control stand, smoking and watching.

A bright orange rescue boat was lowered from the ship to hang just above the floor of the platform. It knocked against the hull. S'Jin took Sabel's hand. Without a word, the scarred man began lifting the younger children onto the boat.

"Sabel, one of us should go up with the little ones," said Reya.

The unscarred man pounded twice on the hull and the rescue boat went up. S'Jin waved to the rising children. From where they were standing, Sabel couldn't see what happened next. She didn't hear any cries for help.

Sabel looked at S'Jin, who was still looking up, now at the empty rescue boat knocking against the side of the ship. She suddenly noticed how windy and loud it was on the open water. She wiped the spray from her neck and stopped. It felt like someone else's neck. Her short hair after the cut. S'Jin was also covered in spray, his school shirt dotted and damp. He reached for her hand and held it tightly, staring at her. She was staring at the men.

The unscarred man spoke something into the ear of the scarred man, who nodded, threw away his cigarette and moved across the platform toward them.

Why was the rescue boat not coming back down?

Couldn't they all have fit?

And where were they going, anyway?

The scarred man's hands were out in front of him, spread wide like a dog catcher's.

Sabel took a step back.

"Stay where you are!" he shouted.

She kept moving back, pulling S'Jin.

"Stop!"

Sabel saw the other two men look up from their work and rush toward them. The driver carried a coil of rope. She turned to call for help and was knocked over by the rescue boat, lowering down. S'Jin stumbled back and let go of her hand and fell into the water. Sabel screamed, and the scarred man dove in. The unscarred man lay flat at the edge of the platform while the driver stood beside him, ready to throw the rope.

For the longest, longest time, nothing happened.

Then the driver threw the rope, the unscarred man got up and both pulled. Sabel went to the edge and saw the scarred man holding the rope and kicking water and holding S'Jin, who was kicking water and kicking him.

The unscarred man pulled S'Jin out of the water and dumped him into the rescue boat. Giving a wide margin, Sabel climbed into the boat and sat down next to S'Jin. She pulled him close to her, startled at how cold and wet he was, and then held his shivering body closer.

The back of her neck tingled.

She felt someone come near, close behind her. It was the scarred man, also soaking and shivering and breathing hard. He was very close now. She didn't turn.

"Do you think someone saves my children by sending them away? Do you think anyone even thinks about my children? Turn around, you little sugar diamond, you—"

"Come on!" called the unscarred man from the bus. "Leave it. We're late for the next pickup."

The scarred man didn't move.

"Now!"

Sabel held S'Jin, cupping her hand on his jaw and squeezing so that he couldn't turn. The scarred man spat and banged his hand against the ship's hull and was still vowing terrible things when the boat went up and blue-gloved hands reached out and pulled Sabel and S'Jin away.

2

Sabel woke when she fell against Reya. She held her breath and waited, but Reya didn't hit her in the ribs. She didn't even make the angry noise in her throat like when the two of them shared the wall side of the sleeping mat at home.

In fact, Reya didn't make any noise at all.

She wasn't moving.

Sabel held her breath. She put her wrist up close to her sister's face, like she was asking Reya's mouth to tell her the time, just like Amma had taught them.

Children. Look at me. Watch my hands. My hands. Watch what they do. This is what you do, if you have to.

This is how to check if someone is alive or dead, without anyone else knowing, even the person.

They had taken turns behind the house, under the trellis, in the times when it was still covered in green and not ash, playing a game Amma called Checker and Checked. How fast it became a contest between them. Many contests. Appa getting mad and telling them to stop playing the fool and listen to Amma. Amma telling them, telling Appa.

No, please, play the fool, but when it's time, know the difference.

And so they had contests to see who could play-the-fool-dead for the longest time. Like holding their breath in the underwater games they would play with the children of other friends of the president, in the crescent-shaped pool at the Patriot's Club. Their parents on the patio, holding glasses the colour of bloom-flowers, laughing.

How many lives ago did they have such pasts and such futures?

On the bus, Sabel waited with her wrist near Reya's mouth.

She waited. Just to make sure.

Yes. Her wrist felt warm and gone, warm and gone. Reya was breathing. Reya was alive.

Sabel breathed out.

When had *she* started holding her breath?

She looked around. Where were they?

The others were all sleeping too, side by side, row on row.

How were they back on the bus?

When did it happen?

And who were these other children, all with the same shaved heads, the same red bumps behind their ears.

They're all jabbed so they don't get the sickness, she thought.

Wait.

This isn't the same bus.

The trees outside were tall and narrow and the branches full of black-green leaves. Here and there, between them, brightness and blue, sky and sea.

Was this even the same country?

"Reya. Reya! Wake up!"

Nothing.

Sabel leaned close and growled. She jabbed Reya in the ribs.

Reya woke up and looked around, wild-eyed and counting her siblings.

"We're all here, we're all here," said Sabel.

Reya looked around again. "There are others. And it's not the same bus. Not even the same country. Sabel, where are we?"

Wherever they were, their old world—falling down or not—had ended. A new one was all around them. Was it also falling down?

S'Jin stepped into the aisle and tugged at Sabel's shirt.

"Come and see. There's a boy hanging outside my window."

Sabel pulled S'Jin to her, and Reya took him and turned him toward her and covered his face—something else Amma had taught them to do the morning after ash from a nearby bomb first fell on the trellis. Both of them looked out their window. S'Jin bit Reya's hands to break out of her hold, and pointed.

They saw legs, arms, a face, stretched and straining.

The boy was about Reya's age.

He was alive.

He was dark and ropey and wearing cut-off school trousers and an open shirt and a loose black tie. Like a noose. He was holding onto the inside frame of the bus window beside which Tric lay sleeping. The hanging boy's feet were braced against the nearest wheel well, and he was smiling.

He's smiling.

He was smiling at them.

At Reya.

"Sabel, who is that boy? What is going on? What's happening?" said Reya.

"He's riding our bus," S'Jin said, amused and impressed, the same moment they heard a thudding and banging and slamming on the roof of the bus.

The bus stopped, and they watched the hanging boy's legs swing out over his head and come down near their window—lots of cuts and scrapes above black boots, tightly laced—and swing again as his hands let go. And then he was gone and then—BANG—he was on the roof.

"How many are up there?" said S'Jin.

"There's people on top of the bus!" said Tric, from the seat behind them.

S'Jin sighed.

By now all the other children inside the bus were awake. Verlane and Theri were sitting across Sabel, their heads down and close together, holding their breath without any contest to win, eyebrows crushing.

Sabel knew in her heart what they were wondering and worrying about. She was wondering and worrying the same things.

Where were they? What was happening?

"QUIET!"

A young man from the front of the bus walked down the aisle

toward them. He held a long black metal pipe. The children sat still and silent. Some were shaking. Others bowed down and against the back of the next seat, bracing for the first blow, arms crossed to protect the head and neck and get it in the ribs instead.

Their parents must have taught them what to do, Sabel thought.

Only one child was doing something else. A little girl with hair like cut bramble, wearing a dress the colour and shape and quality of a garage rag. She had wedged herself in between two seats, her forearms propping her up, and was swinging her legs with great longing, like she wanted to join the boys jumping on top of the bus.

The young man stopped. He planted his feet. Sabel saw his forearms tense, the muscles moving like bellies of snakes, feasting.

He gripped the pole with both hands, breathed in, and rammed it into the ceiling.

"That's going to hurt his hands," said an older boy, watching from a seat farther back.

The young man did it again, and again, walking slowly up and down the aisle. He kept ramming the pole upward, over and over, denting and bending the ceiling, until crusted eyeholes opened here and there, letting in a creamy white light. It was a bright, high cloud day.

And this had been done before.

Finally, he stopped.

He dropped the pole and bent over, clutching and wringing his hands.

"See?" said the older boy watching from farther back. No one paid him any attention.

In fact, no one said anything.

Then came a slamming sound from the roof of the bus, like horses racing hailstorms.

The young man let the pipe drop to the ground. Sabel couldn't tell if it made any noise. Turning to face the front, he put one leg behind him and leaned forward with the other. He put his hands on the top of seats and clutched.

"Do it!" he said to the driver.

The bus began moving, slowly at first then very fast, and then it stopped suddenly.

The children slammed into the seats in front of them, a few of them screaming."

Only the young man didn't move.

Boys fell from the roof of the bus in front and at the sides, tumbling and rolling. One grabbed onto the bus's side mirror, and the driver opened his window and rapped the boy's fingers with the handle of a screwdriver. The boy yelped as he dropped.

He ran and joined the other boys who had been jumping on the roof, all of them massaging and dabbing at their cuts and gathering themselves in front of the bus, yelling and shaking their fists in the air.

"OBA! OBA! OBA!"

Off to the side, one boy lay sprawling on the ground. He wasn't moving.

Is it Reya's boy? Sabel wondered. *He isn't really her boy! He smiled at her once.*

But Reya banged on her window.

"What are you doing?" said Sabel.

The crumpled boy moved a little, and one of the others saw him. Still chanting "OBA!" the boys drifted over to the side of the bus, picked him up and carried him away from the road. A couple of them stopped for a moment and tried to see inside the bus, picking out the driver and the man with the metal pipe. They looked confused, even scared.

Meanwhile, inside the bus, the young man picked up his pipe and came up to Reya. "Why did you do that?" he asked.

"Do what?" said Reya.

"Bang on the window. You banged on the window. Why did you do that?"

"Of course she did that!" said Sabel.

He turned to her instead, smirking.

"Why?"

"The same reason you make noise when you see a wild animal coming close. To make it go away."

It took a moment, but then Reya understood what Sabel was doing and began nodding in agreement.

"Do you want to know what I do when a wild animal comes close?" asked the young man.

"No," said Sabel.

"I do!" said S'Jin.

"He just thinks he does. I know what you do," said Tric, leaning forward from the seat behind them. Children all around them were watching and listening.

"What do you think I do, little man?" he asked Tric, smiling.

"I know what you do. And afterward, you wash off the pipe."

The young man stopped smiling, studied Tric, and went to the front of the bus.

"Did your father do that to the shark you caught on your birthday?" said S'Jin.

"No. Not to sharks," said Tric.

He looked out the window.

Probably remembering faces best forgotten, thought Sabel.

They drove on, a long while and uphill the entire time. They only slowed down at bends in the road, where, beyond jagged low walls made of chipped bricks and old rocks, all you could see, as far and wide as every child on the bus could look, was water—the blue-black colour of coal in sunlight, of bruises the next morning.

At these bends, the driver shifted gears and the engine coughed and gasped. The bus shook and moved very slowly but kept up with the steep uphill climb. Sabel thought about the old judge, last seen on the bridge back home. *Where did he go? Did he send his children somewhere else?* If Sabel had known she was trading her parents for a towel of warm bread, a bus ride and a boat and a jab and another bus ride, she would not have gone. She would have stayed with them, no matter what, no matter who came to the door next, what dropped on the roof next. What mattered was that they were together. With Amma and Appa. Not like this: together, but without them. Which wasn't together. She hoped the judge and his grandchildren were at least together, wherever they were.

"Where are we?" S'Jin suddenly shouted. "Where are they taking us? I don't care if this whole mountain is made of kind guards and candy, I want to stay with Amma and Appa. Doesn't everyone want to go back to their Amma and Appa?"

No one answered S'Jin, but many of the children on the bus nodded to themselves. Sabel told Reya to sit beside S'Jin, who tried to push his sister away. He didn't try very hard.

At the next bend in the road, Sabel saw Theri cover her ears with her hands. Her foiled bit of chocolate fell to the bus floor as she leaned forward. Verlane leaned over and picked it up for her sister and spoke to her quietly.

"Is she feeling sick?" asked Sabel.

"The bus sounds make her feel bad."

Sabel leaned over to help, but Verlane nodded her back in place and looked over at S'Jin and Reya, blank and sad. "I'll take care of Theri," she said to Sabel.

Sabel nodded her thanks. Taking care of Theri gave Verlane something good to do, to keep away her own bad thoughts.

Wherever they were being taken, the route was all trees, the same kind, long and narrow trunks thick with branches, like fistfuls of giant leafy pencils. The children gazed out the windows for signs of where they were.

Of who else was there.

Everyone's ears were straining for when those strange OBA-chanting boys would land on their bus again. But they never did. It was all trees and rocky bends. Now and then, the children, their hearts rolling around like beads of mercury, saw roadside fruit stands and butcher stalls. But they were empty or shuttered, broken in here and there by hungry animals, hungry people, the OBA boys, the weather and whatever else was out there.

The bus finally slowed down and then stopped in the middle of the road. The door opened. Some of the children got up. Others ducked down. Still others tried to push into the backs of their seats, bracing themselves against being taken again. The bramble-headed girl in the garage-rag dress was still swinging her legs and staring out the window. Had they been swinging the whole time?

"Sit! Wait here," said one of the two men at the front.

He got down from the bus and walked toward three rounded slabs of stone sunk into the ground in the middle of a dirt pathway that began at the side of the main road.

Sabel remembered what the scarred man had said to her before she and S'Jin were taken up into the ship and checked over and given jabs behind the ear. They must have slept at sea then, until they were carried and put back on a bus. The scarred man had said that no one was taking his children away from everything falling down. Had the same thing happened here too? Was this man visiting his children's graves? Sabel couldn't see any names or markings on the stones.

But the man didn't stop before the stones. He went past them, into the woods.

"Sabel, I have to go pee too," said S'Jin.

"Remember, you're our sister," Reya whispered.

"So then how do I pee?" said S'Jin.

"Earthquake!" Tric said, pointing at the gravestones suddenly sinking into the ground.

But the bus wasn't moving, and the stones were descending in an orderly way. They weren't marking graves.

"They're blocking a secret path," guessed S'Jin.

The man came out of the woods and motioned to the driver, who turned the bus onto the path and drove over the sunken stones. The man got back onto the bus, and the stones went up again.

They drove on, very slowly, the bus taking up the entire pathway, which, past the first stand of trees, eventually became a wall of red rock on one side that curved upward. On the other side was the same low brick and stone wall they'd passed at bends on the way here, beyond which was the endless dark water.

"Let's go! Everyone out," said the pipe man.

After each child got down from the bus, some thirty in all, they were made to step to the side, near its front wheel. One of the men from the bus counted them and made notes on a pad of paper. Sabel noticed that his tongue stuck out from the side of his mouth while he wrote, such was his concentration on a task not normal for him.

The children were led into the courtyard of a very old building made of red and orange stones. It reminded Sabel of glorious days, days that had been like every day in the time before. The building resembled one of the places with green and white statues where their parents used to take them for family photos and melting ice cream, before her parents would travel to those night parties in northern cities on the president's plane. Marygirl would come to these places with them and wait in the hotel rooms to hear about the places they had visited while she washed off the dirt and stickiness and put them to bed. This was long before her parents told Marygirl she couldn't come with them to their house in the country, and Marygirl of course listened and of course wouldn't listen and, after they drove off, tried to come anyway. On foot, from the city, when it was falling down. Cars and buses and trucks nearly running her down, and Marygirl knowing not to ask for a ride and not knowing even how to find them, and at least that time Amma and Appa told them the truth. That they didn't know what had happened to Marygirl.

A woman was waiting for them in the courtyard.

She was not smiling.

She was wearing a collared white shirt over baggy black soldier pants and tall black boots.

She motioned for the children to approach her.

They didn't move.

She was thin, with light red hair pulled back in a ponytail. Whoever she was, she must have been in charge of whatever this place was. Otherwise, why wasn't her hair short to show that she didn't have the sickness? She had lots of freckles and big, fishy green eyes and thin lips and strong teeth. Along her jawline, her clavicle and shoulders, bones stretched through freckled white skin.

She looked like a large furious child.

"My name is Chynoweth. How are all of you feeling after such a long journey?"

No one answered.

"You are very, very far from home, and you don't know where you are, and some of you, maybe many of you, don't even know why you are here or who I am. Who agrees with what I have said?"

Most of the children nodded.

"You will understand more soon. But first, I just asked you a question, and I expect all of you to answer it. It will be answered before any other questions are asked or answered. We need this understanding, between us, before anything else. And so, I shall try again. How are you feeling after such a long journey?"

A little boy raised his hand. He was almost the same age as S'Jin and Tric and had reedy black hair cut in a perfect fringe across his wide forehead. The hair along the sides of his head and in back was gone. He was wearing a necktie that someone had cut, high near the knot, near the neck. To free him from something, or warn him from something?

"Yes. Please, go ahead," she said.

"I am feeling, Miss, really, that I have to go to the bathroom, please. We were on the bus for a long time. Where, please? Soon! Very soon!"

An older boy cackled.

No one else made a noise.

Sabel and Reya and Verlane and Theri immediately surrounded S'Jin.

The air felt heavy with threat, like that moment before summer rain.

"Sis, I can't believe you've already started! Without me!"

"Hello, brother," Chynoweth said to a large young man approaching them from the school.

He laughed and put one of his big arms around Chynoweth's shoulders, squeezed, and looked at the children, nodding.

For a moment Chynoweth's face showed something—pain that was more than physical—but a moment later she had slipped out of his grip and was standing apart.

"Everyone, this is—"

"I'm Gyre! I'm Chynoweth's brother. Who thinks I'm her big brother, and who thinks I'm her little brother?"

"Who thinks this kid's going to wet his pants?" the cackling boy said.

A few giggles this time, including from Gyre, who had darker hair than his sister and darker eyes too.

They didn't look much alike.

Are they really brother and sister? thought Sabel. *Or are they playing brother and sister? Why?*

Gyre approached the cackling boy.

"That's a good joke. Good joke. Where's the boy who needs to go?"

The little boy with the fringe stepped forward, dancing a little.

"I can take him over there. May I?" said another older boy, staring at Gyre and pointing to some bushes behind the bus.

"You may," said Chynoweth.

"Sabel, I can go with him," said S'Jin, surrounded by his sisters.

"No!" Reya whispered, turning to him.

"You're not allowed," said Verlane, softly. "Amma and Appa

said you're our sister now, S'Jin, remember? How can you go with boys?"

"My friend also needs to go. May *he* go too?" said Tric, to help his friend, and to help himself—because just like that, S'Jin, breaking through his frantic, grabbing, whisper-screaming broken circle of sisters and catching up with the other boys, was no longer their sister.

He's once again Tric's friend, not our pretend sister.

Gyre was standing in front of the cackling boy.

"Do you want to make a new joke now?"

The cackling boy stared into Gyre's dark eyes, like he was looking for fish in a pond, and shrugged.

"I know what it costs to be here. I know what kind of parents we all have. You probably do too," said the cackling boy. "We know they can't do anything to us except keep us safe. So go, like your little sister says."

"You don't think I can do anything to you?" said Gyre. "Really?"

The boy rubbed his fingers and thumbs together.

"Ghee," explained S'Jin, pointing, as he and the fringe boy and the older boy returned from behind the bus.

The older boy stepped in between Gyre and the cackling boy and slowly began to move backward.

Chynoweth came and put a hand on Gyre's shoulder, who seemed genuinely surprised by this. Gyre and the cackling boy nodded and grinned at each other.

"You're brothers?" she asked the two boys, standing side by side.

"No," they said together.

Chynoweth stepped back, glanced at Gyre, and then smiled. "So then. Who's hungry?"

All the children raised their hands, including the cackling boy and the boy who was not his brother.

"Follow me."

Going into the building, Sabel noticed gashes on the outside panels of the arched doors and on the thick timbres stacked on either side, just inside the threshold. She looked down and saw notches, not gashes, cut into the stone floor—where thick timbres had been set up to brace the door against whoever was gashing and trying to get inside. At the end of the tunnel-like entry was a second set of heavy doors, also open.

Those doors were covered in metal sheeting that had been dented many times. They had no knobs—there was no way to open the second doors once you got through the main doors or got trapped between them.

How old were those gashes and dents? What kind of place was this?

But then Sabel noticed something else. The smell.

Food!

Warm food!

The children followed the smell quickly into a high-ceilinged, stone-walled dining hall that had long wooden tables and benches. Black iron chains hung down, ending above each table in round, dusty glass balls with dead bulbs. Narrow windows appeared at repeating intervals on three walls, with thick iron mesh bolted over them. Light still came through. Grey light.

Light that the sun would give off if the sun were made of gunmetal. The fourth wall had no windows but instead a tiny balcony, with an even tinier door visible behind it. Long, black sword-tipped flagstaffs flew scraps and tatters. Sabel could barely make out the faded letters separated by black smudges that ran in an arc under the balcony.

"YOOL? What's YOOL? Is that the name of this place?" asked one of the children, an older boy.

"No. Not the name," said another.

"Then?"

"It's a warning."

"Warning? How?"

"Those other marks are blacked out letters," the warning-minded boy said, pointing. "But I bet it all spells 'If you don't do as we say, yool be punished.'"

"You can't spell, or count. There's not enough marks for all of those words," said an older girl, listening.

The warning-minded boy shrugged.

He's probably seen enough to know when a warning is a warning, Sabel thought. *It's always better to think something is a warning and be proven wrong, than to think something isn't a warning, and be proven wrong.*

"I don't care what they're warning. I just want to eat," said another boy.

The children all looked over at a table that had just been pulled to the side of the entrance. On it were steaming trays of rice and beans and cabbage. The young man who had been in charge of the bus served out food on shiny metal trays, with silver spoons and cups and rough-cut squares of old cloth.

Sabel and her sisters and S'Jin and Tric sat down among the others and prepared to eat. As they did at home, they held hands and began to pray. Theri reached her hand out to the unknown girl sitting beside her.

"What are you doing? Do you think you can have my food? You can't have my food. You have your own food. Stop doing that. Don't touch me. Sickness, no sickness, doesn't matter. I won't touch you. Try it again, and I'll tell my Papo and then you'll see. You'll see!"

Theri pulled back her outstretched hand. She seemed to be counting her fingers, as if to make sure all were still there. She was stunned. Who didn't pray before a meal?

"Theri, what did Amma tell us?" said Verlane. "Only hold hands when you trust them with your life!"

"Are you saying my sister can't be trusted?" the girl across from them asked.

"Enough, Verlane. Theri, here. Theri! Here! Give me your hand," said Sabel, reaching across.

"What are they doing?" the girl sitting beside Theri asked her sister.

"Making a game chain! But why did she want to play it with you? You're no good at games or chains," said the slightly older girl.

"No! They're prain, dummy!" said the boy sitting on her other side, who was older than them both and otherwise looked the same. They were a brother and two sisters.

The boy leaned across his scowling sister and caught Sabel's eye. They were the same age. "That's what you call it, yeah? Prain?" He pointed up.

Sabel nodded.

The boy nodded.

He made a point of waiting while they prayed.

Afterward, the boy caught Sabel's eye again.

"Prain girl, what do you think this place is?"

The children sitting near them who had finished eating looked at Sabel.

"Her name is Sabel," said Verlane.

"Don't tell them our names!" said Reya.

"His name is S'Jin," said Tric, pointing across from him. What else could the sisters do to him at this point?

"I'm Jaka. These are my sisters, Gem and Perdite."

Reya began naming the rest of them. Jaka waved his hand for her to stop.

"Too many! All of you are one family? Your parents must have been mega with ghee."

"No. They still are," said S'Jin. "Not mega with ghee. Just, they still are. Right, Sabel?"

"Yes."

"Sorry sorry. Didn't mean anything, okay?" said Jaka.

Sabel nodded.

He leaned in, looking directly at Sabel. Speaking hard truths, eldest child to eldest child. "But what do you really think, prain girl? About this place?"

"I don't know yet. What do you think?"

The boy leaned back and licked his spoon, shrugging.

"Maybe it's a school. Maybe it's a prison."

"We've lived in both," said Perdite, grandly.

Jaka shook his head, trying to look embarrassed by his sister's boast. He failed to look embarrassed.

"Why would our parents send us to a prison?" asked Reya.

"I don't know your parents. I just know mine. My Papo once took us to prison with him."

"What did he do?" asked Reya.

"Not him. It's what our Big Papo was going to do to Papo and to us—" said Perdite.

"Family talking is for family talking!" Jaka exclaimed.

"Fine. Then why did Papo send us here?" said Gem.

"Don't you remember what he said? After that dirt man took us out of the trunk and—"

"Family talking! Family talking, Perdite!" Jaka said again. "Gem, I tell you every time you ask. Papo sent us here because, whatever this place is, it is safe for us. And you all know it has to be better than our home place. Our home place was like the end of the world."

"Same," said Sabel to Jaka, who nodded while their siblings leaned in to overhear what the two of them knew that they didn't.

"Which place is our home place, Jaka?" asked Perdite. "Big Papo's house or the prison with just Papo?"

"She's right," said her sister. "The end of the world is a nice and pretty answer for people like them. Makes them feel like we're all the same. But when Mamo—"

"Don't say it!" said Jaka.

"Say what?" asked Gem. "Say something about Mamo?"

"I said NO! Don't say it!"

"Do you really think Mamo is still trying to get us back from Papo?" Perdite asked.

"Not her. She doesn't care about us," said Jaka.

"Only Papo cares about us," Gem said.

"No," said Jaka, quietly. "Big Papo wants us too."

He said it in a way that made his sisters stop talking.

The other children stopped talking too.

Chynoweth and Gyre came into the dining hall. The young man at the serving table banged on the trays to get everyone's attention.

"We'll see if this place is better than home or prison or the end of the world," said Jaka. "Or just another prison at the end of the world."

All the children looked up from their empty trays, wondering the same thing.

3

CHYNOWETH GAVE A BRIEF VAGUE SPEECH. The dining hall was quiet.

"Questions?"

No one raised a hand.

"Then we can start?" said Gyre.

Start what? wondered Sabel.

To delay the answer, one child raised a hand, and then another and another and another, until everyone's hand was raised.

Gyre nodded at Chynoweth. "Please keep your hands raised until your question is answered," she said. "When it is answered, lower your hand. So first, there are no exceptions. Your parents will not come to see you here or retrieve you, because they cannot come here. They don't know where you are, only that you are with us."

Many of the children lowered their hands.

"Next, yes, they have agreed to this. They agreed in sending you here that they would never know your location and that this was for your safety and the safety of everyone else in this place. They also agreed that under no circumstances—no circumstances at all—can there be contact between you and them while you are staying here. Again, this is for your safety and the safety of everyone else. The ship will return for you. You will leave here and go to where your parents have requested that we send you. And no, I do not know where you will be sent, only that we are all together, here, until then."

Sabel felt exactly half-relieved at this news.

Then every child's hand shot up.

"Ten days," said Gyre. "You are here for ten days only."

Ten days? thought Sabel. *Would Amma and Appa send us so far away for only ten days?*

Some of the others still had their hands raised. Gyre motioned for Chynoweth to continue answering the children's questions.

"Let me see if I can answer the other questions you have," she said. "On the ship, you were all checked and jabbed, and your hair was cut. None of you has the sickness."

Three more children lowered their hands.

"Next, you cannot leave until you must leave, and at that point, you cannot stay. You have to go back."

Two more children lowered their hands.

"In the meantime, because of what I have told you, you are protected. Protected from what? I think each of you can answer that."

Chynoweth's voice fell away on the last sentence. Like she was speaking to them while being dropped down a hole.

"There are more questions. Look up!" said Gyre.

She looked up and nodded.

"I see there are still some of you with questions. Let me take care of those now. First, we are not the only people living on this island. Second, other than the man who brings us meals and diesel—who is not to speak to you and is not to be spoken to—you will not see any of the other people living on this island and they will not see you unless something has gone very very wrong. Third, when you are not inside during the day, you may move about the grounds as you like. Only, you are never to go into the tall grasses beyond the high playing field. If you go into the tall grasses beyond the high playing field, you are no longer considered protected. You will be found, and not by us. By the others. And I want you to understand me: you do not want to be found by the others. And yes, your parents also agreed to all of this."

Three hands remained raised. A small-boned girl and the two boys who were not actual brothers but still sitting beside each other—the cackling boy and the kind boy who had helped S'Jin.

"What if we get sick? Or hurt? Are you a nurse and a doctor?" asked the small-boned girl.

"You got the jab on the ship, didn't you?" said Gyre.

"You can get sick and hurt from more things than the sickness," she said.

Gyre shrugged.

Chynoweth nodded. "Yes, you are right. We will do what we can, should something happen. Next question."

"My friend the joker has a question. Sis!" said Gyre.

"Ask," she said, twitching slightly, like someone had just slipped a drop of cold water down her back.

The cackling boy stood up.

"Who are the OBA boys?" he said.

Gyre sighed loudly, shook his head, leaned over, and whispered something to Chynoweth. She nodded.

"The OBA boys work for the others," Gyre said very slowly.

No one asked who the others were.

"You may hear them calling to you if you go near the tall grass."

"And what are we supposed to do if that happens?" asked the cackling boy.

"What do you think you should do?" Chynoweth asked.

"Tell you. No. Tell him."

"Very good!" said Gyre.

The cackling boy smiled like he had a mouth full of sweet cream and sat down.

"Also, never join them," he said from his seat.

"Wrong. You won't join them," said Gyre. "You can't. You'll just be taken by them."

Silence.

Gyre whispered something to Chynoweth, who nodded again.

"A final question?" she said to the boy now standing beside the cackling boy.

"Yes. Who are you? Who were the men on the bus that brought us here? Who were the people on the ship? Who else is here, other than you? Why should we do any of the things you are telling us? Where are the others who used to live in this place? What is this place? What kind of place is it? How did you come to be here? Why are there dents on the front doors? Who made those dents? Where are they now? Who are you?"

"And what's YOOL?" asked the warning-minded boy, without looking up from his tray. Neither Gyre nor Chynoweth heard him.

They were both staring at the boy standing beside the cackling boy. Gyre made a show of letting Chynoweth answer first.

"Is it not enough that we are the ones your parents chose, to keep you here?" said Chynoweth.

She doesn't sound like she believes this herself, thought Sabel.

The cackling boy said something that only the other boy could hear. Whatever it was, it made him kick the cackling boy. The other boy kept standing, waiting for more from Chynoweth.

"It is enough. It has to be. This is what's been agreed to," said Chynoweth. "And so it has to be enough, until we get to go back to our parents."

"We?"

"You," said Chynoweth, wincing. "You."

The boy was about to say something else.

Gyre walked over to him.

"Let me guess your next question! Who are we? You want to know? You really want to know? We're the ones who broke through the front doors. Understood? UNDERSTOOD? Why aren't you all nodding at what I have said? Nod!"

The children nodded.

Sabel could feel it about to happen, the way you could feel a storm about to happen. Young and old, they were all about to cry. She didn't know what Gyre would say to that. Or what he would do. But she didn't think he would be gentle or kind.

Nor did Chynoweth.

"Everyone, please, look at me now. Meals are over," she said. "Bring your trays back to the table. Then go back through the dining hall doors, turn right and walk to the first door on your left, which leads to the inner courtyard. Wait there."

"That was going to be my question," Reya told Sabel as they lined up to return their trays.

"What was?" said Sabel.

"OBA."

"Why? Why was that going to be your question?"

"She liked him," said Verlane. "She's worried about him. Because he kissed her window and then fell off the bus."

"No! He did not kiss my window!"

"Who?" said Sabel.

"No. Not exactly like that. But he did fall, remember? It's okay to worry about someone else," said Reya.

"No it's not. You should only worry about your own," Jaka said.

Sabel and Reya and Verlane all looked behind them, surprised that someone else had been listening to their family talk, the whole time.

"He's right," said Verlane.

"What do you know about anything?" Reya said. "You're too little. You won't even go upstairs to close the door, remember?"

"You're both right," said Sabel, looking at Reya and then at Jaka, who nodded with a serious face that was trying to hold back a smile.

"So now these two are getting married?" said Perdite.

◆ ◆ ◆

Sabel hadn't given the address of their country home to a smart boy from the military academy. She'd met him beside the tribute to new martyrs in the president's oceanside park. They'd both been selected by their schoolmasters to stand for the future of the nation during that week's speeches.

He had liked her sash. She asked him if he knew what colour it was. He said red. She said no. He said burgundy. She said no. He said wine. She laughed and said "amaranth." He tried to say it and couldn't, and they laughed and practised. Then he asked her where she was going to be when school was finished, what northern city?

She told him that yes, they were going to a northern city but just before school started again, and that they would be at their country house for the dry summer.

Where? he had asked. He told her that his family had a country house too.

And he told her where it was. Then he waited. So she told him where, and smiled. And he smiled. Not so far apart, when your fathers give your mothers second drivers for dry summers in the country with all the children.

But Marygirl, who had been standing there, was ready to take Sabel to the car, and Verlane was standing beside her. She must have asked Marygirl to come with her, or more likely Verlane had been terrorizing the others in the car until they had asked that Marygirl take her outside. Or both. Probably both. Because Verlane, standing beside Marygirl, studying Sabel and the soldier boy, smiling—both were smiling—was smiling too. Sabel had to pay Verlane in treats not to tell anyone, or the others would pay her in treats to tell them about Sabel's new boy.

But then the world fell down.

And now they were here.

And next? What would happen next?

As Chynoweth had instructed them, the children walked from the dining hall toward the inner courtyard, along a gloomy corridor with plain walls—portraits and other shapes had hung here before, you could tell from off-colour lines and the odd remaining nail. They came to a metal door that led into the courtyard, which had been freshly painted white. Opening the door, they could smell the new paint, like lime and cream.

Why was it painted so recently? Sabel wondered.

Crowded together with the others, Sabel looked up and all around the little square in the centre of the building.

There's only one way out.

Having eaten a meal, she was more awake now, more intent upon making sense of the situation.

The building had three floors, with repeating sets of windows, suggesting rooms above on the second and third. The first floor was all walls save for the narrow door they had gone through. The windows on the third floor were boarded over and painted the same white. Beyond that, it was all sky, the sun hazing through inked clouds, like the day was lazing toward a storm. Inside, as the children looked around, all Sabel could see was stone—no trees, no benches, only a short diagonal brick structure in the middle, a well, with wooden beams holding a canopy overtop.

I wonder what kind of creature might live in such a house, she thought. *Is it sleeping? Would it wake up and climb out and be friendly, or hungry?*

Gyre walked through the crowd and stood beside the well. He looked back at the door. Standing there were the two young men who'd brought the children by bus. He motioned for them to come forward and handed each one a white envelope, which they pressed and felt. One sniffed. Both nodded and tucked away the envelopes.

"Ghee," whispered Tric to S'Jin, who was standing beside Sabel.

"Remember who told you about ghee?" said S'Jin.

Gyre pointed at the well.

The pipe man pressed his hands against its top. He called the other young man over and together they slid the top away. It fell against the side of the well. One of the young men climbed onto the lip, swung his legs in and slipped down. With three sounds, he disappeared. Thump, ting, whoosh.

The other followed. Thump, ting, whoosh.

The children gasped. Chynoweth motioned for them to approach and they peered in. The well had been fitted with a metal slide, its surface almost perfectly smooth but for a couple of notches near the top.

Sabel strained to hear any noises from the bus men who'd gone down, but there were no sounds coming up from the silvery darkness.

"Sis, I bet the children are wondering what's on the other end of the slide."

"Who wants to know?" said Chynoweth.

Even the cackling boy didn't raise his hand.

"What money did you use to pay those men?" an older girl asked.

"Whose money?" asked the girl beside her.

"No," said the older girl. "I don't care whose money. I want to know what money."

Gyre laughed and clapped.

"Well done. Very clever, hiding your real question inside another question. If you knew what money, then you'd know where we are, right? Well, I can do the same, with my answer. I paid them in money they can use where they are going."

The girl crossed her arms and scowled.

Chynoweth and Gyre picked up the well cover and slid it back in place.

"It's time to assign rooms. Boys stay in the north and east wings. Girls stay in the south and west wings. There are bathrooms in each wing. Gyre and I have rooms beside each other, in between the boys' and girls' areas. The rooms have three beds each. Boys, go to the far side of the slide to be sorted. Girls, go to the other side. When you go back into the building, Gyre will hand out your kits. If you came here with members of your family or friends, and you would like to stay together, that's fine. There will be another meal later today. After everyone is counted, you will go to bed. You will be woken up early tomorrow, and after you are counted and have the morning meal, we begin. Okay, let's move, please."

Begin what? Sabel wondered. It didn't really matter, so long as they stayed together and were safe for the next ten days before going . . . where? *Would they go home to Amma and Appa? Somewhere else, where Amma and Appa were waiting? Or just somewhere else, somewhere else, somewhere else?*

Sabel pulled her sisters and S'Jin together and moved them all toward the walls with the other children. Only one child remained near the well.

It was the little girl from the bus with the bramble hair and garage-rag dress. The one who had lifted herself up in her seat and hung there by her forearms when the OBA boys were jumping on the roof of the bus.

When the way was clear, she ran. She reached the well and pulled the false top partway open, jumped up, slipped down, again dangled in place by her forearms, looked around, looked down and disappeared.

Thump, ting.

Only a few children noticed. They cried out and pointed and approached the opening. Walking fast, her face colouring and crumpling like a burning leaf, Chynoweth moved them away.

Gyre glared at Chynoweth. "You've already lost one, Sis. You better hope she wasn't *the one*."

Looking away from Gyre and also from the well, as if not wanting to stare down any child-eater's throat, Chynoweth slid the heavy top closed and motioned to the children around her.

"Okay, let's move please. Back to the walls. Boys to that side, girls to the other."

"Do you think the bus men are bad people?" one of the children asked aloud.

"What will they do with that girl at the other end of the slide?" another asked.

Chynoweth looked at Gyre, who motioned for her to answer. He looked amused and keen to see what she was going to say.

She swallowed. "They don't know she's coming. They are probably already gone. I don't know who will be there when she comes out."

"Maybe she'll be all by herself?"

"No. She won't be," said Chynoweth, in a way that stopped the questions.

"Sabel, ask," said Reya.

"Ask what?"

"Three beds. We are four sisters."

"We're four sisters now. Not five," said Sabel.

Everyone glared at Tric, who had ruined Amma and Appa's plan for S'Jin to stay with his sisters.

"Do you even want to stay with him?" Verlane asked S'Jin, still glaring at Tric.

"All of you, be quiet," Sabel said. "Just wait here a moment. I will ask her."

"S'Jin, you want to stay in my room, right?" said Tric.

"Who said ghee first? Who taught you ghee?"

"Okay," Tric said.

"No. Who?"

"You did."

"Name me like a loud man would when he loses the fight to the bigger man."

"S'Jin taught me ghee! S'JIN TAUGHT ME GHEE!" yelled Tric. "Now will you stay with me?" he asked, lowering his voice.

"Okay. I'll stay with you."

"Thank you," said Tric.

"That's also called ghee," S'Jin said to Jaka, who nodded, a little impressed.

"Sabel. Sabel! Wait!" said Theri.

Sabel turned back. "What? I have to talk to Chynoweth."

"Tell her that Verlane can have my bed. I am the smallest girl," said Theri. "I will sleep beside any of you, or on the floor or under a bed. I don't want Verlane to sleep somewhere else. Verlane can have my bed."

Sabel looked at her youngest sister's face and could tell Theri had just made a supreme sacrifice. The first time in her life she could have a bed of her own choosing and she chose to give it up, to Verlane of all people.

Verlane, who had been listening, gave Theri a hug, slipping the foiled bit of chocolate into her pocket as she moved away. Sabel saw all of this and felt proud of her little sisters. She wanted to tell Amma the next time they had a free moment together, away from others' hearing. Sabel couldn't decide whether it was a good idea to plan for that next time or a dangerous idea. For now, she had to make sure about their room.

"Prain girl! Wait!" called Jaka.

"No. She has to go see the headmistress about us staying together," said Reya.

"No she doesn't," said Jaka.

"Why not?" Sabel said, turning around.

Jaka motioned her over. "Let's do a deal, you and me," he said.

"What deal?"

He gestured toward Sabel's group: Reya, Verlane, Theri, S'Jin and also Tric, and then he pointed at his own: Gem and Perdite.

"You are four girls, including yourself, and two boys. I am one boy and two girls. They say it's three to a room. You take my sisters, and I take your brothers."

"Only one is my brother."

"So you don't care about the other one?"

"That's not what I meant. He's S'Jin's friend."

"Then do we have a deal?"

"Yes. Okay."

They nodded at each other.

"Gem, Perdite, go with her, with . . ."

"Sabel," all three sisters said.

"With Sabel. Boys, you come with me. I am—"

"Jaka," said S'Jin and Tric together.

Sabel nodded, Jaka nodded and the children went to their walls.

They were assigned the last rooms, and they were also the final children to leave the courtyard. Which also meant they were the ones who heard the tapping sound.

"The top is moving!" said Perdite, pointing to the well.

"Is someone in there?" Tric said. "The bad men climbing back out?"

"No, I bet it's the girl," said Verlane.

The top was lifting and closing, lifting and closing.

Gyre saw the children looking at the well and followed their gaze. He called to Chynoweth, and both came over, Gyre holding a stone block.

"Children, leave the courtyard."

Ignoring him, Jaka went to the well. More tapping.

"Don't open that!" said Gyre. "That's how you can get killed! And not only you!"

"No," said Jaka, looking at Sabel and the other children. "This is how we do more than merely stay alive."

Everyone became very still at his saying this.

Everyone except Gem and Perdite.

Jaka's sisters snorted and fake clapped and pretended to move a bow across a violin for the dramatic turn of his words.

Jaka scowled and walked over and angrily pulled the false top over to one side.

The little girl climbed out and stared at the group of them.

Gyre went over and peered into the hole and then looked at her in wonder.

How had she climbed back up? Sabel wondered. *Was she trying to escape and changed her mind? Was she just testing things for when she really will escape?*

Gyre was still studying the girl. Keeping some distance from her, he replaced the cover over the well, set the stone block he had been carrying on top, and walked off.

"You were not here for the assignment of rooms. This means—" Chynoweth started to say to the girl.

"She can stay with us," said Verlane.

"Agreed," said Perdite.

"I'll give up my bed for her," Theri whispered to Sabel.

"Verlane would never let her sleep on the ground."

The girl kept quiet, but when Verlane and Perdite and Theri motioned to her, she followed Sabel across the courtyard, as if from nowhere and nothing special.

4

SABEL WOKE AT DAWN. The sun was a sudden bright white before it went into grey cloud.

There was a knock at the door and Sabel opened it eye-wide. Chynoweth was standing there. Sabel could see Gyre knocking on the nearest door. The not-brother of the cackling boy opened his door. He leaned out and both he and Sabel made like they hadn't seen each other.

"Wake up the others," Gyre said, pointing all the way down the hall.

Sabel and her sisters put on the kits they found in their room—black pants and shirts and running shoes—and then, each carrying a white notebook and green pencil, went to the dining room for breakfast.

Sabel went over to where S'Jin was sitting, beside Jaka. Tric sat on Jaka's other side. Jaka's sisters sat across from their brother and his two new lieutenants. Beside them was Verlane and Reya and Theri. On the far end sat the jumping girl, who had yet to speak. Sabel wasn't sure if she'd actually gone to sleep the night before, lying as she did on a blanket on the floor between Verlane and Perdite and Gem in their narrow beds.

After the meal—cold rice and beans and cabbage, served by an old man who never looked up—the children were sorted by age. Sabel and Reya, Jaka and the two boys who were not actual brothers were sent through the front door, back to where the bus had first brought them. A few others, about the same age, joined them.

Gyre was there with a long black bag at his feet.

Sabel wanted to search the land and sea and sky, but the bus was blocking her view. The weather was heavy and grey.

"You're with me this morning," Gyre said. "Outside. After the midday meal, you'll be with Chynoweth, inside. Then I will do this with the younger ones. So, to begin. Any questions?"

Sabel looked around to see if anyone else had a question. She had only one. What did Gyre mean, the day before, when he told Chynoweth she'd better hope the child who went down the slide wasn't *the one*?

But the cackling boy raised his hand first.

Gyre smiled. He actually looked relieved.

"I think we're all going to hear a lot from you, aren't we," said Gyre, looking at the others as if trying to make friends with them. "I'm definitely going to hear a lot from you, aren't I. What's your name?"

"I am called Theson," he said with heavy emphasis on *The*.

"And that's not your brother, standing beside you, right? Mr. Questions, I call him."

"That's right. His name is Herson."

Heavy emphasis on *Her*, with sadness.

"No it's not," said the other boy.

"Then what is your name?" asked Theson. "We'd all like to know. I'd like to know. I'd finally like to know your name . . . after all this time. So tell us."

Herson shook his head.

"Then you'll stay Herson," he said.

"I actually don't care about his name," said Gyre. "Or yours. What's your question?"

"Who's in the black bag?"

He looked right at Gyre, grinning,

"You're not afraid, are you?"

"Of who, you? Why should I be? You're not even in charge. You have to do what your sister says."

"You really think so?"

Theson shrugged, but something in Gyre's tone and eyes made him stop grinning.

"You just volunteered to open the bag. Come."

Theson looked around.

"Anyone want to come with me?" he said. "Or are you all too scared?"

They're all too scared, thought Sabel.

"I'll go" said Jaka. "I've seen worse than black bags."

He approached the bag, leaned down and turned his back to the others, reaching for it quickly so no one would see his hands shaking. He unzipped it. Sabel leaned over to look. From inside the bag, he produced a simple black stick, made of wood and wrapped in tape where you would hold it, whether to walk, throw, play or strike. Sabel saw him reach in again and pull out something else. A folded piece of paper.

Gyre snatched it away.

"What's it say?" asked Jaka.

Gyre bit around his thumb as he read the note.

He made a funny sound.

As in, a happy sound.

"It says 'This belongs to the prefect of games.' That's me! I'm the prefect of games! I'm a prefect? I never even went to a school that had prefects, before they—" Gyre stopped. He looked like he was thinking about something that made sudden sense. He nodded. "Probably all of you went to schools with prefects, didn't you."

Why did it make him so happy? Why didn't he know he was the prefect already? What were the games? wondered Sabel.

Sabel could see there was writing on the other side of the paper still in his hand.

"What's it say there?" Jaka asked.

Gyre turned the paper over and stopped smiling. He nodded to himself and put the paper in a vest pocket.

"What's it say?"

"Nothing," said Gyre, turning the stick in his hands.

"Can I hold that?" said a tall boy with golden, nearly white, hair.

"If you were me, would you let someone else hold this?"

"Yes. Because you're the prefect of games. You're in charge."

Gyre nodded, looking pleased at first, then tensing as he gave the boy the stick.

But the boy nodded respectfully and then stepped to the side. He began swinging the stick around like a fan blade, stopping suddenly and reversing direction, or pulling it under an arm and pulling it out again, or putting it behind him, pausing, then having it explode into a fan in front again. Eventually, he slowed down, then sped up the motions, then slammed the stick down beside him.

"Very impressive. Now give it back to me."

The boy hesitated a breath but handed it back.

"What's your name?" said Gyre.

"Daveedov."

"You're the one who said the pipe man's hands on the bus were going to hurt, right?" said Sabel.

Daveedov nodded.

"Why? What happened on the bus?" said Gyre.

No one answered.

"Did something happen on the bus?" he asked.

"Something happened . . . on top of the bus," said Jaka.

Gyre nodded. "OBA?"

Everyone nodded.

"They're dangerous, understood? They wait for you in the tall grass."

"So you know them?" asked Sabel. "How long have you been a teacher here?"

"I'm not a teacher," said Gyre, sounding both insulted and embarrassed.

"Then what are you?"

He snorted, and his face went blank, almost worried. "I am . . . I am the prefect of games, remember? So, Daveedov, who taught you that stick work?"

"My older brother."

"And?" asked Herson.

"He won medals."

"And?" asked Jaka.

"They took him on tours."

"And?" asked Herson.

"He swam in three oceans."

"Really?" said Reya.

"Yes!"

"And?"

"They still took him when the fighting started."

"So he lost. He wasn't any good when it mattered. Where is he now?" asked Theson.

"Where do you think he is *now*?"

Daveedov said the last word like it was a curse.

Theson looked at Herson, as if for help.

"He didn't mean it, Daveedov," said Herson. "Sometimes he means it. Not this time."

Daveedov nodded.

"Does anyone else want to show the prefect of games what they can do with their stick?" asked Gyre. A pause. "No? If not, let's put it to use my way. Follow me."

They followed him past the bus and back toward the main road. After a short distance on the old stones, Gyre went into the woods. Walking near him, Sabel saw a pathway leading into a dark cool forest and followed him onto it. Herson and Theson and the others followed from behind. The trees were tall and had no low branches. The ground was soft and damp and matted in fallen greens, with crisp browns that crushed and snapped under footfall and jabbing stick. The children could see a great distance in all directions. It looked all and only the same as where they were. Straight ahead though, through the trees, past Gyre and his walking stick, something looked different. A dark off-blue light. The sea.

Before it, sharply: the edge.

The edge of what? Sabel wondered. *Of where?*

"Who do you think Gyre is?" she heard Herson ask as he came up beside her. Jaka, Reya and Theson followed, just off to the side.

"What do you mean?" said Jaka.

"He means, Gyre obviously went to a school with no prefects," said Sabel. "He was going to say he was someone, something else, but then he stopped."

"I knew my sister would know," said Reya. "Now, Sabel, tell them."

"Tell them what?" asked Sabel.

Reya's face, her eyes, became so wide, so open, so free of guile and full of trust in her sister's knowledge, she seemed surprised she had to explain this to Sabel.

"Tell them, Sabel, why he stopped, and why he sounded funny when he said he wasn't a teacher," said Reya.

How should I know? I thought. But I answered, anyway.

"He stopped because he's keeping things from us."

Theson stopped walking. "Really, you think so?" he said.

"His sister is the one who knows what's really happening," Sabel said. "She just sent him outside and told him to keep us busy until the next meal."

"I'm so glad we have such brains here," Theson said.

"Hey, why do you want everyone here to think you're the worst?" asked Jaka.

"That's what you have to do, when you know what people really think about you," said Theson. He stalked off a few steps, then stopped and turned and looked at them. "And do you know why that is? Ask Herson. He'll tell you."

"Okay. Why does your friend want everyone here to think he's the worst?" asked Jaka.

"He's not my friend."

"Or your brother," said Sabel.

Herson nodded at her.

Herson had a narrow face, wood-coloured like hers, not cream-coloured like Theson's, or black like Jaka's. His eyes were dark and round and sad.

If we were walking down a street, would people think we're brother and sister, or would they think we were— Sabel stopped herself.

She was in a place she didn't know, with people she didn't know, taking care of her sisters and three other girls she didn't know. How dare she care about some stranger boy's sad eyes. Nice eyes!

He was also thin, with long limbs. Appa would have called

him a saloon of a boy. Sabel winced.

Not would have, but would.

He would call him that.

Appa would, because Appa still was. As was Amma.

Sabel wondered why they were here for only ten days. Was that really enough time for them to find a way out of the falling-down world for the whole family? Could Appa and Amma become doctors in northern cities? Or were the northern cities falling down too?

Herson walked ahead to join Theson.

"He's keeping things from us too," said Reya, pointing at him.

Sabel nodded.

After a long walk through the woods, they came to a clearing.

Gyre turned around to face them.

"Okay. If you keep going along this side, you'll come to a small hill. At the top is a playing field and the tall grass that she warned you not to go into."

"You mean your sister?" said Reya.

"That's right. My sister. Chynoweth. You can go up there now to take a look, and tomorrow when we meet outside we'll go there to play a game. And because, as you know, I'm the prefect of games, I'll pick the game."

Jaka raised his hand.

"Would you like to pick the game?"

"No, I want to know what you used to do."

"Used to do?"

"Before you became the prefect of games here, which we can

tell makes you so excited, and also, it looks like, a little surprised. Right? And you already told us you're not a teacher at this school. So what were you before? Who were you before?"

"You first. What were you? Who were you?"

"I can answer those questions," said Jaka. "What was I? Who was I? Same as I am now. The firstborn son of a powerful man—"

"And where is he—"

"Sorry, but I wasn't finished. What I was going to say," Jaka continued, squaring up in front of Gyre, who was smiling sourly, "is that I am the firstborn son of a powerful man who is in trouble just now, and who is going to win in the end."

"You think so?" said Gyre.

Jaka nodded.

"Now what about you? What do you think, prefect of games?" asked Reya, her arms crossed. She looked at Sabel, who was nodding at her to stop talking, so Reya's eyes moved past her. "Also, why are we here for only ten days? Our parents wouldn't send us away on such a dangerous journey for only ten days."

The other children began making noises in agreement. A few were kicking up dust on the ground. Sabel had by now figured out that all of them had—or once had—powerful men for fathers and powerful mothers too. Both. As well as other relations. That's how they had all been sent here in the first place, like her and her sisters and brother. But this Gyre was the one in charge now. And they were in the woods, far from anyone else. They had all been raised around such men—big and strong, yes, but also born and raised and paid for and lined up at dawn to do as they were told, or if they didn't do as they were told, lined up for other reasons. Such were their fathers and mothers.

And here they were, being told what to do by this sudden prefect, this obvious helpman.

"Same as him," said Daveedov. "Not my father anymore, but my uncle. Very powerful."

"So's my mother!"

"And my father!"

"And my aunt!"

"My eldest sister!"

"You're all just sugar diamonds," Gyre said, still smiling sourly.

But again his face went blank.

This time it was like a steel door had just dropped in place.

"You all want to know what I was, who I was, before?" he said, his voice going up in volume. "Really? Really?"

Up and up.

"I can tell you who I was, what I was, what I did—what I did!—and we can go back and put away the stick and then you can go to sleep tonight and the rest of your nights knowing all of who I am and what I did. Knowing that I'm down the hall. That I'm right down the hall, tonight. Or we can walk in the woods and play games on the field until it's time for you to go home to your all-powerful fathers and mothers. Who must be winning, yes, and this is why you were sent here. To us. To protect and prepare you. Right? Right? And don't ask me, never ask me about my father and mother. Because you won't like my answer. Trust me. Or don't trust me. Either way, I'm right down the hall, tonight and every other night until you're the taken."

Taken? thought Sabel. *Taken? Not returned? What did this mean?* Whatever it meant, the way he was talking to them, looking at them, didn't make her want to ask any more questions. *The rest of the children must feel the same way.* She looked at the others. *They were no longer so ready to be so many against one.*

"Now do as I say. One at a time, walk to my left," Gyre said, pleased by the silence. "One at a time. When you get to the place, it's a steep drop, and if you try to go down that way, trust me, you won't be escaping. You won't be anything at all. So let's go, one at a time. And at the place, hold the stick like this, and stand like this."

He stood at soldierly attention, the walking stick beside his shoulder.

"This is called ready pose."

No one moved.

"LET'S GO!"

Sabel did as asked. She took the stick and, holding it straight beside herself, stood where he pointed, looking out to the sea.

"What do you think?" Herson asked Sabel when she returned.

"I think we must be on an island," she said.

"Maybe the tip of our land?" asked Reya.

"No. That water isn't like our water."

"Mine either."

"It's so blue it's black."

"Where I'm from, the water used to be so clear that in the morning you could see even the small fish from the servant's roof," said Herson.

"Oh," said Sabel.

"Why were you on the servant's roof? Did your parents let you go there?" asked Reya.

Herson didn't answer at first. But eventually he told Sabel, quietly and quickly, that he was the son of the servant who worked for Theson's mother. Herson's mother had raised the two boys together. When the falling down of the world had started, Herson's mother used all her money to send him here with Theson.

Sabel said nothing, but she nodded.

Jaka came in close and jerked his thumb backward. "We're being measured with that stick. So they can see how tall we are."

"Who?"

"Exactly."

5

TWO MORNINGS LATER, Chynoweth stood in front of them on a raised wooden platform, behind an old table that held old books. Behind her were four arch-topped windows in a semi-circle looking out toward the water.

The windows were shuttered.

Her day was organized like this: wake up, count off, first meal, then lessons in this classroom for the younger children while the older children were outside with Gyre. They switched at midday, after the second meal. When the afternoon lessons were finished, the children had free time until the third meal, which was followed by final count-off, and then everyone was sent to their rooms until the next day.

On that first full day in the classroom, Chynoweth had opened the shutters and let the light come through, the fresh air.

It gave her hope to think that she was seeing and hearing the same things, breathing the same air as her father, who was elsewhere on the island.

She had kept the windows open until she noticed that the children were getting restless, seeing the dark and empty water. How long until they began asking questions again? Questions that, without Gyre beside her, Chynoweth might actually answer.

In fact, no matter the question they asked, this was the answer she wanted to give: She wasn't really in charge of keeping them here.

She was being kept here, with them.

But if she gave them that answer, and Gyre found out, then what would happen? Not just to her, or just to these children, but to her father.

And so she closed the shutters and passed the morning hours and then passed the afternoon hours with made-up stories and lessons—the old books on the table in front of her were in old languages she didn't know. Her father would have known. Not the languages, but the worth of them. Useless knowledge, useless worth.

The same was true of many of the books in the little library beside the dining hall that smelled like a cellar. She had seen some of the children looking through them, before and after meals, when the games with paper and sticks and forest nuts finally gave out, and so too the dares to bend body parts beyond their design.

They turned to books when they tired of telling and listening to stories from each other, stories meant to impress, entertain, scare—distract teller and listener alike—searching for something, anything to read and send the mind anywhere but here, even for only a page. But the books were in languages they didn't know. A few had drawings in them—these were like food to the starving. The children would make up story after story about the pictures: where this cartman was going with that look on his face; whether the look was guilty or sad, sad or tired, guilty and sad and tired; why that donkey wore a crown and that monkey a gown; how big was the person whose hand held that many planets; how small was a baby who sat on a soup-spoon; what kind of mouth would eat such soup. Those books were looked at and looked at by a few, while others would check the shelves after every meal, just in case familiar words suddenly appeared overnight, or since midday, or after the evening meal, or after the children were sent to their rooms.

That was when Gyre would come to Chynoweth's room for their nighttime sessions about plans for the next day. He would remind her to tell him if she saw anything strange, and remind her why. Otherwise, the plans remained the same and all the days were exactly alike until the days were done: morning and afternoon sessions, each child counted and accounted for to start and end the day, and—Gyre's own idea—each child taken to the edge of the clearing and made to stand against the measuring stick so that Gyre's men, watching from below, could mark down details for each child. If they were even watching, Chynoweth wanted to tell Gyre, this was a useless exercise. From such a great distance, what could they possibly see about each child that they could tell the powerful man coming to get one of them, if he asked for proof before he arrived? But doing this every day, she could tell, gave Gyre something to do that felt real while they all waited for what came next, for who came next. And if someone like Gyre didn't have that, what would he do instead for that real feeling?

Not read, she knew. Chynoweth had a small hoard of books in her room, which she had been permitted to bring when she was taken to the school to act as the children's teacher. Gyre had checked each of them for any weapons hidden inside. Not finding any, he had been confused as to what use the books would be while she was teaching the children. The books were in a language the children would know, and she had planned to share them, to give the children somewhere to go, in their minds and hearts, other than the places they had been, the place where they were now and wherever they would be taken next. But Gyre didn't care—he didn't think anyone would want any of the books. She hadn't shared them with the children yet. Because Chynoweth knew that the kind of children who would want to read books would be the kind of children who would ask questions she didn't want to answer.

Like, *Where did the books come from?*

Whose books were they?

Where did she come from? Who was she?

This was who Chynoweth was and where she came from:

A week earlier, she had been waiting at a ferry terminal with her father to escape the falling-down world. It was just the two of them. It used to be four of them. After it had become just the two of them, they had used the ghee from selling all their belongings other than a few books and gone to the ferry terminal to see how far they could get on that much ghee. There, two young men approached and her father began to ask them about a ship and the men nodded and took all their ghee and put them on a small boat that smelled of fish and that was set to sail right away. The other passengers appeared to be similar in kind to the young men: bullet-headed and seeming to want to race you, not chase you, to prove something about themselves that the falling-down world had, at last, given them the chance to do. When Chynoweth and her father realized they were the only passengers, her father asked if she thought she could swim to shore. Whether she could or not, she knew he couldn't, and she wasn't going to leave him with such men, but her father wasn't going to leave her with such men either. One of them had been watching and approached. The man gave back her father the ghee he'd paid, but her father informed him that he would never sell his daughter. The young man told him it wasn't like that. He told her father that the young men had been asked to watch a group of children that would be arriving at a school on an island. They were to keep watch over the children and protect the island, until the person paying them to do this job arrived. At that point, Chynoweth and her father would be free to go wherever their ghee could take them.

"So you want us to watch the children?" asked her father.

"No."

"Then?"

"She will watch the children at the school. And you will stay with us in the camp."

"Why? If you're making us do this, let us do it together," said Chynoweth.

"No. You'll tell the children."

"Tell them what? That they're being protected by brave young men?" said her father.

The man smiled and shook his head.

"Good try, old man. I don't believe you, and the children won't believe you either. We put a father and daughter together, they'll be able to tell."

"Tell what? And anyway, won't the other teachers at the school tell them?"

"There are no other teachers at the school," said the young man in a way that made her father put his arm between her and the young man.

"You're not brave," he said.

"That's right. And you're not staying with your daughter when we get to the island. Now, just do as we say."

"But I'm not old enough to be a teacher," said Chynoweth. "How many children? I don't know how to do this."

"None of us knows how to do any of these things, but we are all doing them. Also, you're not doing it by yourself."

"Then with who?"

"Your brother."

Chynoweth and her father drew back from him.

The young man grinned and turned to the pack of bullet-heads behind him on the boat's deck.

"Gyre, come meet your sister."

And so she met him, and they were both told what they would be saying and doing at the school even if she hadn't ever been a teacher, a military cadet, or a tour guide, couldn't drive a bus, and didn't have children of her own. Even though she'd shuddered when Gyre was first introduced as her brother, Chynoweth was grateful they would pretend to be brother and sister, not something else.

He slept in the room beside hers.

At night, he stayed in there.

And he was an idiot, a thug, an ass. But he had not been bad to her by word or hand or even eye.

Chynoweth knew this wasn't the case for so many of her friends. A few, whether for their parents or younger brothers and sisters or for themselves, had found their way out of bad places by being more than a sister to the new kinds of men in charge—men who could change your future by stamping papers and opening gates and magically finding free spaces in full ships.

This hadn't happened to Chynoweth here, with Gyre, but she never forgot: he was one of the bullet-heads.

She didn't know anything about the small old man who came and went with food and supplies and diesel for the generators. He never spoke to her or even looked at her or the children.

Was that on orders from Gyre's men? She didn't believe Gyre when he said that those OBA boys worked for some other group. From what she could tell from their clothing, they were runaways from this school, from earlier groups who had stayed here when it was actually a school.

How much time had passed since this place was used in the way it had been intended? High-life people had sent their children here for safe keeping from the falling-down world—not realizing that the world had fallen down here too.

Chynoweth knew about high-life people. The OBA boys must have been runaways from then. She knew OBA stood for Old Boys Association. Her rich uncle had belonged to one of those. He'd gone to one of those schools.

Her uncle had managed to get out early along with his family, before people knew about the sickness. Before the new government was broken. By the time her uncle and his family had crossed to a north land, they were all sick. People said the sickness itself felt like the inside of your body was a pot of boiling water, and that your skin was a lid, pressed on top. Their plane hadn't been allowed to land, and they tried anyway and crashed.

But those OBA boys in the woods weren't her concern. Rather, she was aware that Gyre seemed worried about another group coming to take whichever child was so important to them. He had been impressed by her story about why the children were never to go into the tall grass. He had invited her to join their group if she wanted.

She would never do that. She just wanted for this to be over, for whichever high-life child to be taken by whichever high-life father, so that she could be brought down from the mountain to Gyre's men's camp, to her own father, and they could go anywhere else, just as long as they were together. And if acting like a strict teacher and pretending to be Gyre's sister is what was needed for that, she would do it.

Once, she had wanted to be an actor—a dream in the time before the sickness. Before the falling down of the world. Before what had happened to her brother and her mother. And now here she was, whether she wanted it or not—an actor. Her greatest worry was that other, even more bullet-headed young men would come and take over from Gyre's men. In this falling-down world, that kind of thing was happening over and over. What would happen to her father then? What would happen to her?

Also, even if the new men were from the high life, the kind of men that in the before times would never have looked at someone like Chynoweth—who would never look at them in any kind of life or world—what would happen to the children? What could she do? What could she do to protect so many children?

High-life children. The kind of children with more place and money than she had ever had. The kind of children who waited in long cars, the engine always running to keep them cool, while their tall, heeled mothers who smelled of flowers browsed in her father's bookshop for old heavy fancies for their husbands and grandfathers and the dear leader's birthdays, the children climbing around the old lady servant who threatened them uselessly, while their tall, boot-wearing security men who smelled of cigarettes kept an eye out. Those were the kind of children who were here for safekeeping by people who had been removed even before the children arrived.

Now Chynoweth was watching such children, while her father was being held somewhere else.

Gyre had told her that if another group of men came and got through, they would be much worse than he and his men, and that she should trust him about that, and that she should tell him if she ever saw, or noticed, anything or anyone that seemed strange.

She nodded.

But what she wanted to say was, *How could she tell if anything or anyone seemed strange, in the life that was suddenly hers?*

She trusted him about nothing, because she trusted nothing about him.

He was one of them.

And she was not.

Definitely, she was not; nor was her father, taken and kept somewhere outside those shuttered windows.

Before she and her father had gone to the ferry and encountered Gyre and his men, her real brother was taken and bashed repeatedly when he refused to join with the bad men who knew they were bad and would only say they were protecting him from worse men. In the end, they insisted that he join them and fight with them. Or else.

Did all men speak this way, in the time of the falling-down world?

Chynoweth didn't remember men speaking this way in the before-time.

The bad men had laughed that first time they came to her father's bookshop, when her father had tried to buy her bruised brother's freedom from fighting with the most precious things he still had.

Books.

"First editions! Rare editions! Signed copies!" the men had said, repeating her father's pleading words before smacking away his hands and tossing the books to the floor and dragging away her brother. Her mother had been standing in the threshold that led to the family's little apartment behind the bookshop, not making a sound, as if she were screaming and breathing and crying at the same time.

But that wasn't enough. Soon after her brother died while fighting with those men, they came back to her father's bookshop and smashed it with the bricks, they said with odd formality, from the building where her brother lay dead (but when it was finally safe to go to that building, prepared with spray for the wild dogs, the building itself was gone). The men smashed up the bookshop to show the other families who lived down the lane what would happen if their sons were "cowards," like Chynoweth's brother —who was no coward, who had gone to fight. But what kind of fighting could a young man do when he grew up with beautiful old books on folds of brushed velvet? After her brother was gone, and the shop was gone, and her mother was gone—it had been her lungs, maybe from the sickness, maybe from finding herself sonless in the fallen-down world—Chynoweth and her father took what they could carry, sold and traded what others would accept, and left home for wherever the next available boat would take them. They had been in among the crowd with all the others when Gyre's men spotted them—a perfect pair for their purposes.

Chynoweth knew that her brother would have never let this happen.

But perhaps they could all get through these ten days, which was now five days.

But five nights too.

She heard children crying behind closed doors at night—and she would knock, rap her knuckles hard like a government agent, and they'd stop. They'd huff a little, whimper, be told by an older girl to be quiet. She wanted to open the door and go to them, but she knew that if she did, if she broke even a little, the children would know something, and who knew what Gyre would do. Who knew what would happen to them all then?

They had given her a jab in their camp near the harbour before sending her up the mountain to the school, just in case she had the sickness, so that she wouldn't infect the children.

She did not believe Gyre or the other men.

But she wanted to.

Was that enough?

No.

But it was just more than absolutely nothing.

And in such times and places.

Also, before they parted, were parted, Chynoweth's father had hugged her and kissed her head and whispered in her ear:

"Kataba kataba kataba ka."

This was the kind of thing that means nothing unless it means everything, the kind of thing a parent whispers to a child, has always said to a child—no words, only sounds.

Sounds that mean *I love you. I am here. I love you. I am here. I love you. I am here. I love you.*

She had left her father behind and had been brought to this place with that secret sound in her ears.

◆ ◆ ◆

It was a sound that she recalled, like a prayer, in the silent times in the classroom. And by recalling it, she could keep going, as she did the morning of the sixth day, teaching the younger children while Gyre had the older children outside.

"Children, does anyone have a story they want to tell today, or shall I tell another one about animals?"

No one raised a hand.

Chynoweth knew these children from high and faraway places didn't know what had happened here before they arrived, or what was happening while they were here, or what might happen to them, to one of them at least. And maybe they didn't know for certain that whatever the situation was, it was opposite to what their parents had thought would happen in sending them here. But, Chynoweth imagined, most of the children knew, even if none of them would say so out loud. Because then who would do what, next? Instead, just as Chynoweth acted as their teacher, they acted as her students.

But even the best actors and the best students aren't just actors or students.

A girl raised her hand.

"Yes?"

"I want to know something."

"What's that?" asked Chynoweth.

"I want to know who came from the worst place to this place."

The children began shifting around, looking at each other.

"I don't think that's a good idea," said Chynoweth. "I don't think it matters where you have all come from. I think what matters is that we are here now, until it is time to go back."

"But I don't want to go back to my place. Mine was the worst place of all," the girl said.

"No it wasn't," said a boy.

"Oh really?"

"Really."

"Prove it."

"Children! We aren't going to do this."

But the boy stood up and came to the front of the class, very formally. He leaned in close to Chynoweth. All the other children leaned forward, except Verlane, who was asleep because the jumping girl wouldn't let her sleep at night.

"Miss. Let me tell my story. No one will want to tell a story afterward. I promise. I won awards at my old school for speeches and stories. I am good at this. No one could ever do better."

"Do you want to tell it?"

The boy shrugged.

"Go ahead then."

"Teacher and fellow students. Greetings. One day a man with a hammer walked up the path to our house because now it was supposed to be his. We looked out our upstairs windows. Everywhere, we could hear windows breaking and dogs barking and doors being pushed open. We could hear mums screaming and dads yelling, which was really just screaming louder than the mums. Our front door was made of glass. He didn't break it. Probably because it was already his new house and why break your own window? We could see from a bedroom window upstairs that he pulled a screwdriver from his back pocket, pressed it to the keyhole and hammered, and the lock fell and rolled away.

"Then we heard him open the door. He was breathing in a lot. Not breathing like he was tired but breathing in our house smell. So I did the same. Oranges, candles, bread and leather. We started to run around upstairs. Dad pulled a dresser against the bedroom door. Mum called out to God, asking God for help and blaming God for letting this happen.

"The man began climbing the stairs."

Here the boy at the front of the class stopped his speech and stomped on the wooden floor. Everyone jumped, including Chynoweth.

"He reached the bedroom we were all in and began kicking the door. His boot came through right away. The door was hollow. We heard him say:

"'Shabby.'

"He kicked in a second hole, then stepped through it and tipped over the dresser, but by then we were all in the closet except Dad, who was holding the man back with the schooldays bat he kept under the bed. The man took Dad's bat and pulled Dad close.

"Dad was saying, 'No no, please no, just tell me what you want. We have all the—'

"Then Mum ran out of the closet and jumped on the man's back. He stepped backward until they hit the wall over and over again.

"When Mum fell down, he crossed the room to Dad's closet and took out a belt.

"Stepping out, he tied the bedroom shut with Dad's belt, went downstairs and opened our fridge.

"Mum couldn't move Dad.

"Crying, Mum said she had to get me out of there. Up and down the street, we could hear people yelling.

"And no sirens.

"No one was coming.

"I remember Mum and Dad talking once about how the airports weren't safe anymore, that people from the downside of the world were running through them and taking planes and coming to the upside, but not to our city, never to our city, they said when they saw I was listening. Our city is the safe city, they kept telling me.

"They were wrong.

"The man who had come to our house and taken our house was not the only new man.

"The same thing was happening in every house, up and down our street.

"Mum and I watched from the upstairs window as we heard the man downstairs opening and closing our fridge.

"Across the street, another one of the new men was fighting an old man. One had thrown the other through a wooden screen door and he came out after him. They were on the front lawn. The men almost looked friendly after so much fighting. Their heads were on each other's shoulders, they were breathing heavy, their arms moving up and pressing down on each other's bodies, slowly, like they were at a dance. The old man, our neighbour, was wearing blue pajama bottoms. He was much bigger and he went to the gym before dawn every day, and I know from Mum teasing Dad and Dad teasing Mum that all the old man did was lift up and look in the mirror every day. The other one looked more like the new man in our house. He was very skinny and dressed in all black. The bigger man kept hugging him, around the neck. Then he dropped him on the lawn and cursed him and spat on him and laughed at him and went back inside his house.

"A few minutes later, another skinny new man came walking down our street, and when he saw the body on the lawn, he cracked his knuckles and stretched his arms and went into the house. He cracked like this.

"Yes. I guess it was his turn. That was when Mum went to the mirror and wiped her eyes and fixed her hair like she was going to a party. She told me to turn around. So I turned around. Then she saw what I had to see outside and told me to turn around again and close my eyes, instead. So I closed my eyes and when I opened them, Mum wasn't wearing her pajamas. She was wearing her newest workpartydress.

"Mum is beautiful. So beautiful.

"The most beautiful on the whole street.

"She has skin that is smooth as a hotel bed and smells like milk and flowers.

"In her workpartydress, she went into the closet, to the locked box in the back that she didn't think I knew about and took out a key and then bent down to unlock a length of wood in the floor—this I didn't know about—and took out bars of raremetal and left them on the floor. She began calling the man to come upstairs.

"Mum spoke to him without me getting to hear.

"But I saw her pointing at me and at the raremetal. And at herself.

"And I could see the man's face. Ugly face. Smiling face. What an ugly smiling face.

"In conclusion, that's how I got here, and that's my worst place. My home is my worst place. Thank you."

The boy returned to his seat.

The children were silent. Now no one wanted to tell their story or hear any others.

Almost no one.

The girl who had first boasted that she had come from the worst place raised her hand.

"Yes? Do you do you want to give a speech now?" asked Chynoweth, almost more amazed than worried.

"No," she said, about to sob. She swallowed and squeezed back the tears and with rage in her voice said, "But I still come from the worst place."

After what they had just heard from the speechmaker boy, no one wanted proof from the girl. And so Chynoweth told animal stories until the midday meal—stories she remembered hearing from her father when she was a little girl.

6

ON THE SIXTH DAY, at the end of the evening meal, the cook motioned to Gyre to approach. He told him what he had been told to say.

"Kitchen boy!" said Gyre. "Look at me! Look at me and say it again! Tell me the message again. Who gave you the message. Who were they? What did they look like?"

Gyre wanted to see his eyes, to know if the sickle-shouldered old man was lying.

A man like that in a world like this.

Of course he was lying.

More like, what kind of lie was it?

Who was he protecting with his lie?

This wasn't the only reason Gyre wanted the old man to look at him. He was lying to himself too.

Gyre was.

But he could keep that lie far away because the kitchen boy wouldn't look at him.

He only repeated the same thing, again and again: "They are waiting for you at the main road. They said to come tonight, when everyone is sleeping. High moon."

Gyre bit his lip.

"They said 'high moon'?"

He nodded. "High moon."

"Okay. Don't say it again."

Gyre tried to remember if high moon meant something with his latest group. Or did it reach into him from another time, another place in his life?

He couldn't remember. And what good was remembering anyway?

The two of them were alone in the kitchen. The children and Chynoweth had gone upstairs. The kitchen was a room of silver sheets and wooden counters and deep tubs, all of it dented and scored and stained with how many meals made, for how many people, over how many years.

Had this place been a hotel, school, hospital, a healing house, holy house, before the falling down, before it became a refugee camp for rich children, a bank vault of rich children?

Actually, Gyre knew it wasn't any kind of hotel. He'd worked at one, at least outside one, in the time before the falling down of the world. The latest head of his group knew this, which is why he'd asked Gyre to come and stay here with the children until the others came.

His job was to spot, to watch, to guard.

Pretend he was brother-teacher.

Gyre.

Who'd grown up with no sisters, no teachers.

He'd grown up in a great white block building along the sea. The building was nearer the ferry terminal than the city. Not in a hotel but very near a hotel. He and his father, a dishwasher in one of the hotel kitchens, had lived with many other hotel workers in one of the many rooms that had been built into the back of the hotel's old boathouse—a storage place smelling of bodies for stacked mattresses and splintered, spiderful crates, full of repaired radios and left-behind beach toys and slippery magazines of the newest cars and bikes from northern cities, and rusty cookie tins full of playing cards and old photographs, the dining room's day-before clearings and the great hall's banquet leftovers.

Also bottles, always: some full, some empty, some full of cigarettes, others candled.

Many broken.

The only rule in the old boathouse: no women allowed.

When that rule was broken, it never ended well for anyone, especially the women.

If you were a hotel guest, you never asked about that place because the whole reason you spent so much to come to such a hotel was to get to look the other way for a few days.

This was Gyre's wedge of the world, in the time before its falling down.

Here and now, what Gyre wanted until this current job was over was that nothing would happen for four more days, and then the powerful man would come and take the child he wanted, and then Gyre and his men would get ghee, and then Gyre could go.

But go where?

He didn't know.

If this worked to plan, he would be asked to go with this group of bullet-headed young men to whatever was going to be their next job. And the next, and the next, and the next, until what?

Until he would—what?

What would he do instead with his life, if it was still his?

Young men like Gyre didn't know the answer to such questions. Mostly, they didn't want to know. Better just to take job after job after job.

Each one a test for the next.

His father had helped him get started. He admitted that. When he was almost old enough, he became a car watcher in the hotel parking lot, squatting in front of one fancy car after the other, each with more space than the cooks and cleaners and their families lived and slept in.

While the drivers read newspapers and smoked under the shade trees, he had to stay right in front of a car for hours.

For this first job, he wore a succession of hats. The first was made of straw and a little chewed up. He recognized a hat like that from a children's book he had read that showed an old woman wearing a hat like that in her garden; the next one had a green visor that made him think he lived on a different planet when he looked around at certain angles; finally, his most beloved hat, a perfect, brand new black and gold hat with a roaring lion on the front, the mascot of a sporting team from the north—it was stolen from him by the head watcher and sold before he could do anything about it; then a fisherman's cap that looked washed in rust and smelled like gas and sardine tins and was the softest, softest thing ever to touch his head.

His work was to stay like that—squatting, watching, guarding—until the valet came and called the driver and gave Gyre a coin per car. By day's end, most days, he would have enough coins to fill a pocket. Before he could go to the old boathouse, the head watcher and the valets took half his coins. His father took the rest. For safekeeping.

One time he kept his hand in his pocket, his hand closed on a couple of coins his father didn't need to know about just as the valet and head watcher hadn't known about them. Big thin coins from a different world, like the shiny medallion fish you'd sometimes see hanging near the fishing boats, the fishermen trying to get hotel people to go out on the water and catch something from a different world too.

He should have taken his hand out.

He didn't.

His father had grabbed his wrist so hard Gyre had thought it would snap like parts of a broken chair going into one of the barrel fires the men kept going all day when the hotel closed for winter. His wrist ached while his father counted the coins and then gave Gyre back the two big thin shiny ones—then his father left their room with the rest of the coins.

Safekeeping.

He knew his father had left to chance at cards until the coins were gone, and they were always gone before Gyre fell asleep. That one time his father came back early, with a jingling sound still in his pockets, carrying a city of cakes on an actual plate. He must have convinced someone in the kitchen.

The cakes were for Gyre.

An apology, for hurting his wrist.

In turn, Gyre gave his father half of the sweet falling towers. He took a couple of bites himself, then went out for cards again until the rest of the coins were gone.

That was how Gyre learned to trade useless coins for better ones with other watchers, and to keep more and more of the coins in his shoes, his mouth, the back of his neck, his beltline, and also in the splits in his pockets. He moved up fast among the watchers, watching better and fancier cars closer and closer to the front gate, then briefly became the head watcher, then a guard at the front entrance of the hotel that his father—who washed dishes in the kitchen beneath the official basement kitchen—had never, ever walked through. When the main doors of the hotel opened, the air was empty and cold. To have so much money, you come from a northern city to stay inside a colder place in a world of such hot sun! Gyre would watch children coming and going in school uniform for afternoon tea. Wearing luxury masks that were bought, not found or homemade. Shoes shined with butter, the other valets said.

Butter! For shoes!

What perfect lives.

Prefect lives.

But Gyre was doing better too. As a hotel guard, he was getting a little paper in his pockets, not just his cut of little boys' coins.

The day before men attacked the hotel, Gyre was taken to the side of the building by another of the guards, where that guard's new friends were waiting.

Gyre was given three choices.

He would be let go to return to his post and then see what would happen to him.

He would be let go to leave the hotel and run away, and then see what would happen to him on the streets.

Or he could join them. The men were planning to attack the hotel. It was not yet the time of the falling-down world, but attacks like this one, happening more and more, everywhere, were moving the world to its falling down.

The men who were going to attack had such beautiful black boots.

Shiny and dark, and who needs butter when you have steel toes?

They were many, and they were all friends, so far as Gyre could tell.

He could also tell their life plans did not include dying for sugar diamonds or growing old enough to steal pocket change from their sons only to lose it at nighttime games of cards.

And so he joined their group.

And that group became another group, and another, and now, this one.

◆ ◆ ◆

Who was waiting for him at the road? He knew this kitchen-boy old man didn't know. The old man probably thought the best way he could stay alive and still get paid for the work he did was not knowing.

He wasn't wrong, Gyre knew.

But otherwise?

They had never said they would send messages or ask to see him. They only said, stay and watch and guard all of them until we come. Be the woman's brother. Remind her of her father when she needs to be reminded.

So far, she'd gone along with the way things were.

It was working.

No child lost. No child asking too many questions.

Everyone just waiting, and waiting in safety.

A kind of luxury.

Didn't they know this, down the mountain?

Was this a test?

He'd already passed the first, giving each of the lower boys from the bus exactly the money he was given to give to them before they went down through the hatch in the courtyard.

All to show the children that they were the ones their parents had hired to watch over them, a regular and proper operation that hired other people to do things. Drivers. Cooks.

That one child, the little girl who didn't speak, had gone into the hatch and come back out of it.

Maybe she was the one. Maybe she knew?

Whether it was her or one of the others, was this message

from the group good news—had they been informed about which child was wanted earlier than planned?

Or was this bad news? Had his group left and a new one arrived?

If so, would Gyre fight them or join them?

He immediately knew the answer.

He'd join.

Wouldn't you?

They might say they already had exactly the right number of men and then see what he'd be willing to do, to join.

And he would have to fight one of them to join the rest of them.

He would look at the other faces and the first one to look away would be the one to replace.

He'd seen this happen.

Gyre opened and closed his hands.

He'd more than just seen this happen.

"Please, big boss," said the kitchen boy, who was as old as his father, if his father was even still living. "That is all they said to tell you. Someone came to the camp kitchen before I brought the meal here and they told me to say this."

"Has something changed at the camp?"

"I don't know anything, big boss. Only to make the food and bring it and this time bring the message. Please, I must go now. Please, big boss."

"No. You will wait until the others are sleeping and then you will come with me to get this message."

"No. I can't do that."

"What did you say? Are you the big boss now, old man?"

Gyre stepped forward and took the cook by the shoulder and

began to squeeze and push him down to the ground. He went to put his other hand over the man's mouth, but the man grabbed Gyre at the wrist and squeezed with such strength that Gyre thought of coins in pockets and chairs in the barrel fires of winters with his father.

He let go and stepped back.

"I won't, I said. If I don't go now and get down the mountain and to the camp to help get the dinner for the others in your group, the meal will be late. And they will take this out on my wife and daughter. I know they will! I cannot be late. I won't."

"You won't? What will you do then? Fight me?"

"Yes."

"You'll lose, old man."

"I am fighting for all that I have and love. What are you fighting for? Ghee?" The old man was looking right at him now. And not looking away.

Gyre's heart felt as heavy as his head.

There was no way such a small man could do anything to him.

But even if Gyre stomped a dog down for biting him, he knew he'd be limping afterward.

And then what if Gyre actually had to run?

"You will answer to me, if that message isn't what you say," said Gyre.

"It is. I must go now."

"Then go, old man."

That night, after the children were in bed and the moon was making old stones and treetops look silver, Gyre tapped on

Chynoweth's door.

He tapped again.

He pressed his face against the jamb.

He said her name.

He waited.

He wasn't scared.

He didn't care if anyone else knew where he would be going, or why.

But someone should know something.

Because even a nobody is still someone.

Finally, she opened the door an eye-crack.

"I did the counting off and everyone is in their rooms," she said.

"I have to go up to the main road," he said.

"Why?" she said, opening it more.

"They sent a message."

"Who?"

He made a face, like it was obvious to him. Another lie. But Chynoweth nodded. She believed him. Which made it a little easier for him to believe.

"Can you ask them about my father? Can you send a message back to him?"

Gyre made another face. "What's the message?"

"Wait."

"Wait? You're telling your father to wait?"

"No, Gyre. You wait."

She shut the door and Gyre could hear her moving around in her room. He had to go. He should tell her he had to go. High moon. But he waited. She had never said his name before. He didn't even know she knew his name.

Maybe she would open the door with a message for her parents and, like in the shows, give him a lock of her hair, a locket, a lock and key to her love.

Something for him.

Hadn't they been through so much together already?

The door opened.

Chynoweth tried to give him a small square object covered in cloth.

"What's this?"

"It's a book."

"Why?"

"I want you to ask them to take that book to my father, so he knows I'm okay."

Gyre shrugged and looked away.

"What is it?" Chynoweth asked.

He looked at her, making his face look hard for show, hard like the burnt sugar top of the cakes his father used to bring him.

"If I don't come back . . ."

"Why wouldn't you come back?"

He shook his head at her. He knew she blamed him for his group taking her father. Why didn't she thank him for treating her like a sister, sleeping in the next room all these nights?

"What?" she said, softly this time.

"Once, the hotel where my father worked lost power for days and days. This was in the time before. They lost all power. Who knows what happened. I was little, and it didn't matter how it happened. The ice chests were melting. The manager gave the kitchen boys all the fish and cakes, and the kitchen boys invited the cleaners and we all went to the beach and it was night and there was fire and singing and my father danced with a pretty lady and she had a daughter who was much older than me and beautiful and all the boys wanted to dance with her, but she picked me. She picked me and held me on her hip, and she told me I had to protect her from bad men and I said I would and I did and we danced under the high moon and it was the happiest night that ever was. And I have never told anyone that, until right now. And it should be known."

Gyre wiped his eyes and left.

7

SABEL WOKE UP. She heard noises in the courtyard. Bad noises, bad men noises. Gem and Perdite were still sleeping. She got out of bed and went to the window and looked out from a corner, and when she saw what was happening, she went next door, to the room where her sisters were sleeping.

Only, they weren't sleeping. They had also heard the noises.

She turned Verlane and Theri away from the window. Verlane broke free and when Theri tried to break free, she saw just a little of what was happening in the courtyard. But then Verlane turned away from the window. She faced Sabel and put her hands on her ears.

In the courtyard, two men were holding Gyre by the arms. Sabel didn't recognize them, and even if she thought Gyre was a bad man, he was, at least, a bad man she knew. He hadn't done anything bad to them.

Poor Gyre, she thought. *Poor, poor Gyre.*

He seemed to be talking fast, bargaining at first, then

threatening, then begging, but Sabel couldn't hear any of it. The windows were sealed shut. She saw Gyre take a deep breath and begin to scream, but she heard nothing. The two men were fast. They had probably done this many times. One of them tied Gyre's hands with stretchy black bands then opened one up and pulled it down over his face, so that he looked like a common bank robber. The same man then produced a roll of black tape and wrapped it around and around Gyre's mouth. He was pulling and kicking but couldn't break free. They covered his nose and eyes with the tape. The other man took something out of his pocket and hit Gyre in the stomach and chest with it, again and again—very fast—and Gyre began to look like a swimmer tired of treading water, and soon he looked like he was nothing nothing nothing at all.

Holding her younger sisters against her, and grateful at least that the others were still asleep, Sabel saw one of the men open the hatch of the well. They took things from Gyre's pockets and checked his boots and pulled them off and then dragged the body to the hatch and pushed it down. They went over to where they had been standing with Gyre and inspected the ground in the moonlight. One of them took off his shirt and spat and the other spat too and the shirtless man wiped something off the stones.

Blood, Sabel thought. Gyre's blood.

Then the shirtless man nodded at the other man and walked back to the hatch. The other man said something to him and he turned, said something back, thought about it, and put his shirt back on. He climbed into the hatch and disappeared. The other man threw his old shoes down the hole after him and closed the hatch and looked around the courtyard and up at the windows, and Sabel dove down to the floor, pulling the others with her.

Finally, Reya woke up.

The strange and silent jumping girl, Sabel noticed, was already awake. Had she been watching the entire time?

Sabel was breathing hard. Verlane and Theri were too.

Sabel stood up in a crouch and looked out the window into the courtyard once more. It was empty now. Where had the man gone?

She listened for the sound of heavy boots on the steps leading to their rooms.

"What did you see out there, Sabel?" asked Reya in a whisper.

Sabel didn't answer. She just gulped air. Gulped and listened for heavy boots. Swallowed and squeezed tears, and with that she hadn't yet had a chance to wonder about what to do, now that she had seen what those men had done to Gyre, and what she now knew, which was that, however bad Gyre was, he was gone, and someone worse than him was here.

Where is Chynoweth? Sabel wondered. *Is she also watching from her window, scared? Or is she still sleeping? Or is she the one giving the orders?*

After what had happened, would she protect them, or was she one of them?

Sabel didn't know. She did not know. She was the oldest and she did not know.

"Sabel, what should we do?"

"Sabel, should we tell Chynoweth?"

"But what should we tell her? What did we see?"

"YOU KNOW WHAT WE SAW!"

"No she doesn't. She didn't see all of it."

"Neither did you! You looked away first!"

"You cried longer!"

"Shhhh!"

"Sabel, go and tell Chynoweth."

"No! Don't leave us here by ourselves!"

"I'm here," said Reya.

"You were sleeping. You didn't wake up when you were supposed to!"

"Sabel," said Reya, about to cry.

"Reya's here with you," said Sabel, nodding. Reya looked down.

"Then go back to your room before they check," said Verlane. "Or they'll ask why you're in here and then they'll know!"

"They'll know what?" Theri asked. "Do we even know what's happening with those bad men, those killing men downstairs?"

Sabel wanted to tell Theri that she was proud of her—but what a world, this falling-down world, where you tell your baby sister you're proud of her for being clear-eyed about the killers among them.

"Theri's right," said Sabel, watching her sister smile.

How many other times in their lives before now could Sabel have given her good words, instead of giving them here, and now, for this!

"So, Sabel, what should we do?" asked Reya.

The jumping girl crawled over to their side of the room and

rasped, "Don't sleep. Don't scream. Don't sleep. Don't scream. Don't sleep. Don't scream."

8

THE NEXT MORNING IN THE DINING HALL, Jaka noticed that the sisters looked tired, and that they were arguing with each other.

Must be a girl problem, he thought.

But if it was a girl problem, why didn't they ask his sisters, Perdite and Gem, to join them?

A family problem then. And family talking was only for family talking.

That was *his* family rule of law—he respected it with others.

But then, why was their little brother, S'Jin, still sitting with him?

Whatever it was, they were upset and arguing.

Maybe I should send Perdite and Gem to find out.

No. He'd have to bribe them, and in this place, what could he offer? Only the promise of something sweet, shiny, lots of it, spoonfuls and boxfuls, in the next place Papo sent them to, if it was an upper kind of place and not a lower kind of place.

Upper, lower, wherever: Jaka knew what mattered most to Papo was keeping Jaka and his sisters away from Big Papo, their grandfather. Jaka also knew his Mamo didn't really care. She had her own kind of spoonfuls and boxfuls—pills and medsins—that she got from her father, Big Papo. Their grandfather. The most terrifying man in the world. A war-making man everyone called The General.

Not: General.

But: The General.

Both at home and in the northern cities, Jaka's Papo had done good things for bad people and bad things for good people and bad things for very bad people, because he was the marriage-son of The General, a war-making big man.

But then one day Papo told Jaka he wouldn't do anything more to anyone else.

When Big Papo found out, he decided it was time for Jaka to join the family business. This began with teaching Jaka how Big Papo could make people do what he wanted them to do.

One time, when as usual Mamo had been deep in her medsins, grey-eyed, not even able to say hello or goodbye, Jaka had been called to come see his grandfather.

Perdite and Gem were playing in a closet. They were hiding. Probably so they wouldn't be called.

But Jaka had been called, and he knew he had to come and sit beside his grandfather.

He smelled Big Papo—a green and brown and salt smell, like a rusty boat engine eating seaweed. Big Papo held him close and felt him shake as Jaka heard sounds that people should never,

ever have to make for anyone, anything, good or bad or worse. The sounds of Big Papo, The General, punishing people for not doing what he said.

People being destroyed, people making their last sounds of life, while he, Jaka, was held close to his grandfather and made to listen. Big Papo placed cologne hands over Jaka's eyes because, Big Papo said, he was too little to see such things.

So, a little boy listening to those sounds is okay?

Not that he asked the question. He knew the answer.

Yes.

Yes because, sitting in Big Papo's lap in the big leather chair they would drag into the courtyard of the compound for Big Papo, Jaka was told that all this would someday be his. Big Papo's words were wet and hot in Jaka's ears, like oil popping from a pan. The oil being poured on a man begging to be shot.

Everything Big Papo was doing, even right now, Big Papo had explained, was just for Jaka.

Jaka was going to be the next Big Papo, not Jaka's useless Papo, who had been sent to a northern city and then been sent back, tail so tucked he was sucking on it like a baby soother.

Jaka was definitely going to be the next Big Papo, Big Papo had told Jaka.

No he was not, Jaka thought.

Which was why that night, Mamo still in her medsins, Jaka had told Papo what had happened, and what Big Papo had told him was going to happen someday, how Jaka would become Big Papo. How Jaka had heard all this while a begging man was being oil-skinned apart before his very ears. Jaka told his father all this, not as a story, but to ask, "What are we going to do?"

Later that same night, when the compound was quiet, Papo took Jaka and Gem and Perdite and went to live in the prison. They lived there on the promise that Papo would tell judges about all the things Big Papa had done, and after he told, they would be sent far away. But this was only a little sanctuary for them. After a little while, someone else's people or some new group of patriots blew up the prison's side wall and drove in empty trucks and filled them with prisoners and left. Escaping before Big Papo and his men drove in, Papo put Jaka and Gem and Perdite in a giant car trunk that smelled like they weren't the first people who'd been put in that car trunk. They waited in there a long time, the girls finding and holding onto him at his wrists in the dark. He wondered if Papo would come for them or not. Then the trunk opened and it wasn't Big Papo's cologne-smelling hands reaching in for them, as he had worried, but Papo and another man, a panting dirt-man in a guard uniform.

The other man put Papo in the trunk with them and now the trunk wasn't so giant and Papo told them all to keep quiet, that he had given this man ghee to get them out of there. The car sped and skidded through gunfire and voicefire and kept going and going and going. Jaka fell asleep. When the car stopped and the man opened the trunk, they could see it was a normal night, normal clouds, normal stars—not blackout, not bombsmoke, not tracers.

And it was very very quiet.

Wind was coming off the salt-smelling water, swishing through the reeds.

And then Jaka smelled it. Green and brown and salt.

Had the dirt man driving the car found his way to upper living?

Had he sold Papo and Jaka and Gem and Perdite to Big Papo for more ghee than Papo had given him?

Was this the end of everything for Papo, for them with Papo?

Medsins and blood smack and cologne smell?

All of that, and for trying to take away his grandchildren, would Big Papo put Papo down in the pit in front of his latest leather lounger? And would Jaka be made to stand there and listen to what happened next—to his father?

Jaka grabbed Papo, to hold him in the trunk with them, not let either him or them be taken to Big Papo.

But Jaka was wrong.

This wasn't the end of everything.

This was just the next thing: a small boat, floating in green-bladed water.

"You're going to a safe place for children. I will come get you when I find us all a better safe place," Papo had said, hugging them before they got into the small boat and were taken to a big ship, where big ship people in gloves and masks made sure they didn't have the sickness and then jabbed them and sent them here, to this place.

Jaka believed Papo's promise and often told Gem and Perdite, so that they would believe, together, and wait in their believing for Papo to find a better safe place.

That morning in the dining hall, when Jaka saw Sabel and her sisters stop and start their arguing while looking and looking at

Chynoweth sitting by herself at the head table, he figured it out.

He figured out this had to do with Gyre, who hadn't shown up for breakfast yet. Gyre would usually be in the dining hall by now, walking around the tables, taking food off older boys' plates and waiting to see what they would do.

Maybe Sabel and her sisters are debating about whether or not Gyre and Chynoweth are brother and sister.

But did they really think Gyre and Chynoweth were family?

How could Sabel and her sisters think that?

How could family not see not-family?

Jaka leaned over.

"Do you really think they're brother and sister?" he said.

"Who?" said Sabel.

"Gyre and Chynoweth."

Sabel shook her head at Jaka, slowly, as did her sisters.

"They think you're a dummy," Gem said to her brother, with deep relish.

"You have no clue," agreed Perdite.

"So then what's happening?" Jaka seethed, sensing that his younger sisters were right about something, right about him being wrong.

His sisters shrugged and returned to their rice and beans and cabbage. Jaka looked back at Sabel, who was not smiling but was enjoying his little sisters humiliating him. Her eyes were sunken, like she hadn't slept. The same was true of her sisters, he noticed. And none of them were smiling at Gem and Perdite's victory. They all looked worried, even scared.

"So, prain girl, tell me, what's the big deal this morning?" said

Jaka. "Seems like it's to do with Chynoweth. Are you trying to figure out something about her before Gyre comes for breakfast?"

"He's not coming for breakfast," said Sabel.

"How do you know?" he asked, swallowing hard, suddenly feeling like he didn't want the answer.

"He was never late coming for breakfast," said Reya.

"Why did your little sister say *was*, prain girl? Why not *is*?"

All of them swallowed their lips and pulled back, like Jaka was asking them to eat an old friend.

"What are you all talking about? Here he comes," said Gem, pointing to the shape of the young bullet-headed man in the dining hall doorway.

Jaka smirked and shook his head at them for all this drama. Sabel and her sisters and the jumping girl clearly hadn't seen or heard anything about the world as it really was, about people as they really could be to each other, he thought. That's why they were so easily upset.

Jaka shifted around to see Gyre coming late for the meal.

But Gyre was not-Gyre.

Who was this?

What was this place?

Jaka looked at Sabel and her sisters.

"What do you know?"

9

CHYNOWETH TURNED AS THE NEW MAN sat down beside her.

"Who are you?"

"I'm Sidian," he said.

"Where's Gyre?" she asked.

"Who's Gyre?"

Chynoweth pulled back and knocked over her glass of water and was about to . . . but the new man took her by the wrist and pinned it against the table.

"Kataba kataba kataba ka," he said.

"What?"

"Kataba kataba kataba ka."

"What? No. That's not yours. You can't say that. How do you know that?"

"Your father told me to say that to you. That you would know what it means."

"What does it mean?"

"How should I be the one to know? I don't think I'm supposed to know, right? Isn't that it? I only know this: He said you would know what it means. Only you. And come on, kataba girl, you know what it means, right?"

"Yes. Okay. Okay. It means he's still alive."

The new man nodded and got up and went over to the serving table, helped himself to a tray of food and two glasses of water, asked the cook for a rag, then came back, wiped the spill and began eating. By now most of the children in the hall were staring at him.

There was a low murmur.

"Now it's my turn," he said.

"Your turn?"

"Yes. I have a question for you."

"Okay."

"Who's Gyre?" he asked, smiling.

She did not smile back.

She remembered that Gyre had tried to be friendly and easy at the beginning too.

"Gyre was one of you," she said.

"No he wasn't."

"Yes he was. They, your group, sent him here with me, to watch these children until they know which one they're looking for. He didn't tell me he was being replaced. But he said he was meeting someone last night. That was you?"

His eyes narrowed. His face cracked a little. "No. You don't understand. I am not his replacement. I am not anyone's replacement. Do you understand?"

"Okay. Then what are you?"

"I'm the one they sent to stay here until the mega man comes for the child."

"Which child?"

"Does it matter? They will know which one, when the mega man comes."

Sidian drank some water. He looked around and shrugged.

"What does that mean? Is your group still trying to find out, like Gyre said? And as soon as your group finds out, will they come and take that child and then the rest of us can go? I can go to my father? That's still the agreement, yes?"

"No. No. You don't understand."

"No? The agreement's changed? We have to stay longer? How much longer? Why can't my father be sent? He could help! He could teach the children much more than I could."

"You don't understand. It's not my group."

"What's not?"

"His group."

"His group?"

"Yes. Gyre's group. Which wasn't his. There is no way he was in charge and also sent up here."

"Oh. I see. His group. Your group. There was his group, but then your group came. And your group took over."

"Yes."

"And his group?"

"Is gone. Gone."

"Gone?"

"Yes. Gone. Listen to me. No. Look at me when you listen to me."

She looked into his shark blank eyes.

"Forget this Gyre. Don't forget your father. He's still alive. Remember? Remember Kataba kataba—"

"Stop staying that. It's not yours to say."

"Wrong. Kataba kataba kataba. It's mine to say because my saying it tells you that your father is still living, and you want to keep it that way. And keeping it that way means you're going to tell me what we do here until my boys come to finish the job and then, yes okay, you can leave, get your father and go. It's mine to say as much as I want. Kataba kataba kataba."

She didn't say anything.

She breathed out.

She wanted to hear the sounds her father had made for her again, the sounds he had made since she was small. She wanted to hear it from him, alive, with both of them leaving this place. Wanting it filled up the space that otherwise she would have given to feeling sorry for Gyre. She was surprised at how much space she could have filled with feeling sorry for him and wondering where he was now.

"How many children are here? And what are their ages?"

"There are thirty children. Twelve boys and eighteen girls. Youngest is eight and oldest is sixteen."

"Tell me about the days?"

"I take the older children for half the day, and Gyre takes the younger children, and then we switch. Inside with me, outside with him. And when he has them outside, he takes them to a clearing and makes each child stand there so that they, his group, can check each child from below."

Sidian snorted.

"There's no way to tell from down there which child is the one."

Chynoweth suddenly felt sorry for Gyre. He was like a child throwing a fishing line onto the road and waiting for dinner.

No, not a child. He was a bad man. But to Chynoweth, just now, he was not the worst man.

"And the only rule is that no child can be lost, and no child can be hurt until we know which child is the one who's wanted?" Sidian asked.

"Gyre never said it like that."

"So you lost a child? You hurt the children?"

"No! Of course not. Neither did he. But you just made it seem like the children *can* be hurt, after the one is found."

"The only thing they told me, my group, is to make sure no child is lost, no child is hurt, until we know which one is wanted. And that we might never find out until the man who wants this child arrives."

"When? What are they going to do with the child? What will happen to the other children?"

He shrugged.

She bit her lip.

"The boat that brought them here. Is it coming back?"

He shrugged.

"I don't know. I won't care either, once we find the one. And really, what do you care about these sugar diamonds if you get to leave, go back to your kataba kataba? You know these are children of big people. The kind of people who have doctors for their dogs and wrap their trees in blankets for winter. That's not me. Is that you?"

She bit her lip harder.

"They're still children. Maybe the rest of them will go on the ship if it's coming back for them."

"Yes. Maybe. But if we need the ship ourselves, we'll take it. And we might take some of them with us."

"Why? What for?"

"What for! Really? In this falling-down world, you ask what for? For ghee. We're all ghee, kataba girl. People like us, we're spoon drops of ghee at the market stalls. These children? Yes, still children, but they're like gold bricks of ghee, their whole lives spent sitting in silver pots at the banquet table. Now, finally in the world as it should be, we get to sit at the head of the table, just by handing over one brick, and yes, putting the rest on that ship and spending them when we need to. We're all ghee. Only, they're our ghee now."

She said nothing.

"Anyway, until my group sends word that we're to bring one or all of them down to the camp in the bus, we stay here."

"Do you know how to drive the bus? Do you know the code for the barrier that goes up and down, that controls access to the main road?"

He hesitated. His black eyes beaded and quivered a little.

"Yes."

"Gyre didn't."

"I do. What about you?"

"No."

"No more splitting the children by age," he said, his eyes

quivering even more. "I'll take all the boys. You take all the girls. Then we switch. But not yet. Not today. I want to look around first. Also, where do I sleep?"

"The children sleep upstairs, in two hallways, boys to one and girls to the other. Our rooms are in the middle."

"Our rooms are side by side?"

"Yes."

He nodded.

"Okay. So we can talk later tonight. You and me."

Chynoweth made a quick decision.

"We talk after the evening meal, in the library beside the dining hall. Then we go upstairs. I count off the girls and you count off the boys, and then we go to our rooms until morning. All of us. In our own rooms. By ourselves."

He laughed to himself.

"Don't worry, kataba girl—"

"My name is Chynoweth."

"As I was saying, don't worry. I didn't come up here to start a dynasty. Okay?"

"Okay."

He nodded and then shrugged.

"But if we're both here and the nights get cold—"

"No. No way."

"Do you really think you can—"

"Yes. Or try and see what happens."

He laughed a little but then caught her eyes—not glassy, not furious, but hard. "Don't worry. Now, I want you to do something else."

Chynoweth looked at him, fully, for the first time. His eyes were dark like Gyre's, but more blank. Only now did Chynoweth sense that there had been at least something other than shark in Gyre's eyes. Not that it mattered now. What mattered was getting through the rest of this with Sidian, not Gyre, until and unless Sidian too became not-Sidian. Whatever got her back to her father and got them away.

Other than the eyes, the rest was the same—another bashing bullet-headed young man just a year or so older than her, with a broad back and thick arms and flat stomach, wearing dark pants and a dark shirt and the same boots.

Gyre's boots.

Chynoweth's eyes filled with tears. He had come to her room the night before and confided in her, with his story about being a boy at a beach at night, about a dance, the moon. He hadn't been trying anything on her with that story. He had been trying to give her something that was only his, in case the rest of him was lost. Which it was now, because of this man sitting beside her chewing a heel of brown bread. He was the one who mattered now, she reminded herself. Not Gyre. Not her holding his memories. That wouldn't get her father back. She squeezed back the tears in anger. How dare she mourn Gyre, the thug who kept her here. Why was she letting in something, anything about him that was good? That might have been good? Did he deserve that for what he did, in bringing her here, for what he would have done if told to, to her or to her father or any of these children?

But am I any better to these children, just by saying they're still children, against Sidian's ghee plans? I have no idea what will be done to one of them.

But ransom or rescue, if that was the price for her own life and her father's, she would pay it. Was already paying it.

"What do you want me to do?" she said.

"Well, first, keep asking that question, and it will keep you and your father safe. Understood?"

"Understood."

"Good."

He pointed at the rest of the tables in the dining hall. All the children were staring at them.

"Tell them who I am."

"I don't know who you are."

"You can say whatever you want, kataba girl. But you better say it fast, and make sure they believe you."

"What's going to happen to him, now that he's gone?"

"Your father is fine, I already said. Just do what needs to be done and he'll stay fine."

"No. Not my father. I meant Gyre. Where did you take him?"

"Oh, I see. I see. He became your sweetheart boy up here?"

"No. Like I said, I don't want a sweetheart boy. I'm not like that. What's going to happen to him?"

"Nothing's *going* to happen to him, kataba girl. It already happened to him. It happened to him last night. In the courtyard. But don't worry."

"Worry? Worry about what?"

"We cleaned it up and sent the body down the well."

Chynoweth stood up.

"CHILDREN! Attention, please! I would like to introduce you to my cousin, Sidian. My, my brother Gyre had to leave. He will not be returning. Sidian is here now. This is Sidian. I will speak with him for a while this morning and then we will begin lessons inside and outside. Until then, go to your rooms and do your cleaning and washing."

She got up from the table and left the dining hall. Sidian also got up, smiled and waved at everyone, and followed her.

"That's not her cousin!" said S'Jin.

The others stared in silence at the empty head table.

"Or," S'Jin continued, "if that new prefect of games is really her cousin, then, then . . . Tric really caught a shark with his papa and helped reel it in!"

"I didn't actually catch a shark," said Tric. "One of the men shot it from the boat."

Everyone nodded.

10

THAT NIGHT, LYING IN BED, staring at thankfully fixed shadows on the walls, not sleeping, Sabel was thinking about Appa for the first time in a while.

What was he doing, now that he didn't have to shop for gifts and treats?

How did he find a plate of melon slices for her; a towel of warm bread for Reya; a foiled bit of chocolate for Theri; a bowl of plain cold rice for Verlane; a cup of pitted cherries for S'Jin; a bowl of sour yoghurt for Amma; a cup of black olives for himself. A plate of melon slices, for her.

How did Appa find all of that, at the end of the world?

This is how he did it:

He went shopping.

He went shopping at the end of the world.

He managed to find treats for everyone before sending them all away.

The question wasn't, How did he find sweet syrup at the end of the world?

It was, How dare he find sweet syrup at the end of the world! Why find sweet syrup instead of greater sanctuary, for all of them, together? But that was Appa at the end of the world: shopping for treats.

What was he trying to find for them now, Sabel wondered, *while we are here?*

Because this was only for ten days.

Was that why Appa had held out his hands, fingers spread, shaking, as he did when they were getting onto the bus?

Not hitting against an invisible wall, but telling them, with those shaking hands, that this was only going to be for ten days?

No.

Appa always had shaky hands.

Well before the haircuts on the ruined trellis behind the country house, the whole family had known this.

Amma had the steady hands. Amma was steady. Like Sabel was steady. Like Sabel had to be steady even if she didn't know why, or where, or with or against whom.

But was Amma any better, Sabel wondered, *with her wise warning to them?*

"Touch only those you are committed to for the rest of your lives," she had said.

What if S'Jin had listened to Amma's warning, the day they were sent here?

What if he hadn't let the scarred man scoop him out of the black water?

He would have drowned.

The rest of them? They'd still be sitting in a life raft, carried along in the ocean air, the old-city people throwing rocks at them, the rescue boat gone on to pick up the next group.

Amma and Appa thought they were sending them somewhere safe. Probably this was a place they had heard about from others in their high-up rooms in the time before the falling-down world: at the Patriot's Club, at the white sand beach enclosed in green leaf- and cream flower-covered blast walls, at name day parties and in the cold-air eating rooms that backed onto the parade stands cupping the president's bulletproof bell jar podium on military review days.

But all of that disappeared long before our last meal.

Had Amma and Appa spoken to other parents that time the families we knew from the president's house had come to the country house, all of them on their way to their own country houses or elsewhere? Sabel had been trying to listen to the grownups talking while Reya, Theri, Verlane, S'Jin and the other children debated what had happened to the president's zoo animals. There were rumours that they had been hunted down and eaten. By whom? Maybe by the president's enemies, hungry for him and everything he had, or maybe by all the packs of poor people, the street and shed dwellers and ones with the sickness.

Who were probably just very hungry, Sabel thought.

How did Appa and Amma even know about this place?

The judge. It must have been the judge, who used to come and talk with Appa and Amma on the veranda before they left the city.

It had to have been him.

He had wanted to send his grandchildren here, so much that he brought them to the bridge and tried to block the van. But his grandchildren weren't on the list and the bus men had pushed him down and away.

Where are they now, the judge and his grandchildren? Are they somewhere better than here?

Wherever here is? Whatever this is?

To keep them safe, Amma and Appa had sent them here!

To what, exactly?

An old stone building meant for schooling and sleeping, partway up a green mountain, surrounded by dark water.

A place where the children didn't learn much, inside or outside.

Listening to stories that Chynoweth must have taken from secret books.

Walkarounds with Gyre and kicking and throwing balls and tugging on ropes made from found rags.

Rice and beans and cabbage, rice and beans and cabbage.

And then another day passed.

A place where the people in charge didn't seem to know what they were doing, only why: to keep all the children here, until it was time for them to leave.

And then Gyre had suddenly been made to leave, not just this place but this world, his life.

"Remember, children," Amma had told them, their last day together, "what we are doing, where we are going, is because we are hopeful."

They had no idea.

They thought they did. Parents always do, don't they?

But sometimes, they really have no idea.

At least Amma and Appa are safe, she decided, decided to believe.

Safe, and getting ready for the children to return and be safe. All of them, together, and safe. Day eleven.

Sabel was sure of this because she had to be, so she could tell her sisters and S'Jin and they would believe her, when the early morning and late-night questions came, as they did every day, that yes, yes, she promised: "Appa and Amma are safe. They are okay."

In fact, she promised that they were more than okay.

She promised that they were busy, like they used to be, only now they were busy finding a good place for all of them to go, maybe even their old servant Marygirl. That this is why they were sent here, so Amma and Appa could have the time to find a little sanctuary for them in this falling-down world.

But is that really what they are busy with these days? wondered Sabel.

Sabel's lie-awake thoughts turned back to her here and now. To what they would need to do the next day. A group of them had agreed to meet in secret, away from the school, in the playing field. The older boys had asked, through Jaka, for a secret meeting about Chynoweth and Sidian.

Sabel knew Herson was going to be there.

He wasn't like the others.

She didn't speak much to him, but often found him sitting nearby for Chynoweth's storytelling sessions, and nearby, but not exactly beside her, whenever Gyre had them outside. Herson always seemed nearer to her than not, but never too close, like children in northern cities watching snowflakes fall and never catching them because that was when they disappeared.

Lying in bed, Sabel shook her head at what she was thinking and feeling while they were being cared for by either one or two killers. They had to decide whether to tell Chynoweth what some of them had seen the night before.

They would meet in the playing field to talk about whether Chynoweth already knew, which is to say, whether she was also a killer. They had to do this before another night, maybe another killing.

The next day, during free time before the final meal, Sabel and her sisters, Jaka's sisters and the jumping girl walked to the playing field, which was surrounded by woods on three sides. Along the fourth side was the tall grass.

The others were already there, standing beside the tall grass—Jaka, Theson, Herson, S'Jin, Tric and Daveedov, the boy who knew how to hit with a stick. He held a long branch in one hand and with the other was pulling off its leafy ends.

Sabel went to brush the hair back from her ears, only to find she had no hair, just spikes and brindles and warm skin.

Her heart was beating hard, thinking about Gyre, and also about S'Jin. He was standing beside Jaka and Tric. In only a few days he had gone from being her sweet baby brother to a fierce and hard little creature loyal to Jaka.

But her heart was also beating a little strangely, even here and now, because of him.

Herson.

Despite all her worries about her sisters and brother, her worries and anger about her parents, Sabel passed her hand over what hair she still had. *About a boy?* She remembered the only other time she'd felt her heart flutter like this. It was because of that smart boy from the military academy—the one who had told her he liked her sash. And also the word for its colour. Not burgundy. Amaranth. That smart boy had been standing with her on the podium, beside the tribute to new martyrs, the two of them representing the future of the nation during that week's speeches by the president, for the president and about the president.

That was a time and place from a whole other life than this, and he had been a boy. Were that life ever to return, she could imagine Amma and Appa approving.

She wondered what she'd think of that boy now, after all this, seeing him in military uniform.

She was no longer the girl whose heart would flutter because of a boy's eyes upon a pretty sash. Amaranth was just a pretty word.

Instead it was beating like that because of this boy, who, like everyone here, came from a shiny and high place elsewhere. Where didn't matter at all anymore.

Herson was taller than she was, with a long nose and ears that wouldn't have looked so big if his hair were longer. His shoulders looked strong, always a little turned in, like he was making space for someone else. She could tell this was because of the other boy he was constantly with—Theson, who walked around with his chest pushed out, his shoulders pressed back. Sabel had met boys like him many times, at the Patriot's Club and in the president's lounges at ceremonies and parade days.

Boys like him who, when they approached, and they always approached, never ever told their names.

They always told their fathers' names.

And then they waited.

They waited to see how impressed, surprised, scared, excited you were to hear their fathers' names. To know you were talking to the sons of such men, with such possibilities ahead for whichever girl they chose.

All of that, in the smirky smiles, the spiky eyebrows, the endless slow nods.

Until, in such times and places, Reya, standing beside Sabel, snorted. And then the sisters began laughing and turned away, or the boys stopped smiling, stopped spiking their hair, stopped nodding and went off in search of other girls who didn't yet know their fathers' names and knew better than to laugh.

Herson was there now, waiting with the others and not exactly smiling at Sabel as she and her sisters approached.

The children formed a semicircle, kicking the ground and looking into the middle distance.

"Who wants to go first?" said Jaka.

"We're the ones who saw what happened," said Reya.

Jaka shook his head, then jerked his head toward the tall grass. "No. I meant, who wants to go in *there* first."

"I will," said S'Jin.

His sisters leaned in and made to hold him. He scoffed and stepped back.

"S'Jin's not allowed. His sisters say no. Don't worry, everyone," said Tric, beaming, looking right at S'Jin, then Jaka, then S'Jin again. "I'll go first."

Now it was S'Jin who leaned in, ready to take hold of Tric.

"We don't really know what's in there," said Daveedov, turning his stick slowly in his hands.

"That's the point of why we're meeting in there," said Theson.

"I thought we were here to talk about Chynoweth and the new man," said Herson.

"We are," said Jaka. "And what that means is deciding whether we can talk to Chynoweth about the new man. Whether we can trust her or not."

"If we trust her, we shouldn't go into the tall grass, because she told us not to," said Reya.

The children all considered this.

"That's not what she said," said Herson. "She said if we went into the tall grass, they couldn't protect us."

"Protect us from who?" asked Daveedov.

"Maybe from whoever killed Gyre last night," said Verlane.

"What did that little girl say?" asked Daveedov.

"Didn't you see the new guy this morning?" said Tric, sounding less shocked than Daveedov.

"The cousin, she called him," said Daveedov.

Tric and S'Jin shook their heads in elaborate, glorious, pitying ways at how basic the boy's sense of the situation was.

"Last night—"

"Wait! Don't say anything else!" Herson said, interrupting Sabel.

"Why? Do you think we're being watched?" she asked.

The children all looked around the frowsy oval of grass near the scrubby playing field, which had netless posts made of metal gone to orange rust with flakes of white paint.

They were a ten- or fifteen-minute walk from the main building, along a pathway of tamped down dirt. They couldn't see it for the surrounding trees. And if they couldn't see the main building, no one in the main building could see them.

Sabel looked up into the trees.

But the trees had no life in them at all. They were tall and clutching-branched and thick-leaved and birdless.

Have the birds flown somewhere else for the season—or for safety? she wondered.

"Not even any birds in this place. Have you ever been somewhere that did not have birds?" asked Herson, now standing beside her and looking up, not looking at her, not speaking directly to her but, for her, closer than ever before. "There have been a few. But I don't blame them for leaving. Whichever ones got away, got away before it was too late."

Not looking at him, Sabel suddenly felt mad at Herson. This was the first time they'd been this close, but what he'd just said sent her far away.

For Sabel, birds and birdsong were the sounds of crack and moan.

Every year, before the president gave the country the gift of celebrating his birthday, he'd be given a gift, all for himself.

One time, Sabel and Reya were selected to present it to him. They wore their best dresses, the seams of which a female guard unstitched for a security check in one of the side rooms. Amma had to be called to resew them. Then they were given the plate, to carry together. The plate was covered in a towel. It had many small bumps.

Fruits? Sabel had wondered.

Cakes?

Mysterious eggs?

Grand chocolates?

The sisters tried not to giggle and hoped he'd invite them to taste his treat.

They placed the plate before him and stepped back.

He removed the towel and smiled.

Before him was a plate of songbirds.

Two of the table servants came forward and stood on either side of him. They unwrapped a fresh towel and, when he nodded, placed it over his head. Leaning forward, he ate the birds whole, one at a time, under the towel, making long, low, happy sounds as he crunched. Amma and Appa were present, being the president's doctors, in case tiny bones caught in his throat. Sabel and Reya backed away slowly into the farthest corner of the giant blue dining room, but they could still hear the crack and moan.

"Sabel, are you okay? Do you really like birds or something?" Herson asked, still standing beside her.

"What? I . . . no. I don't . . ."

"I'm sorry. I didn't mean to—"

"Hey, lovebirds! Stop whispering secrets and tell us if you see anyone," said Theson.

Lovebirds?

Before either of them could blush and disavow, S'Jin, Theri and Verlane had moved to stand in between them.

"I don't think we're being watched," Herson said to everyone.

"Me neither," said Sabel.

"What about from in there?" said Verlane, pointing.

They looked at the tall grass. Couldn't someone, couldn't many people be in there, watching them, waiting for them?

"If we're going to talk about this, let's do it in there," said Theson. "We won't be seen, and Jaka's pets can play right here and tell us if someone is coming."

"We're not pets," said S'Jin.

"We don't play," said Tric.

"Fine. Jaka's guard dogs. Standing guard. Better?"

S'Jin and Tric looked at each other and at Jaka and then nodded.

Sabel wondered what kind of baby boy she would be bringing back to Amma and Appa.

"You go first," said Jaka.

"I will," said Theson.

Theson didn't move.

Jaka smiled and the little boys snickered and Theson made as if he was about to stomp them, but they didn't move. They waited for him to try it.

He didn't, but he still didn't move any closer to the tall grass.

"The boys are scared, Sabel," said Verlane. "Should we check for them?" Perdite and Gem snickered.

"Send her in. She's not scared of anything," said Theri, pointing at jumping girl.

Everyone looked at her, expecting she might just spring into the air and land in the tall grass, scattering whoever or whatever might be in there.

But she didn't move either.

"We're wasting time!" Sabel cut in.

"Give me that," said Herson.

Daveedov handed over his stick. Herson went to the edge of the tall grass and swung the stick through, bending the yellow-green blades. He took a step and swung again, a step and a swing, a step and a swing.

"Too slow. Someone could duck," said Daveedov. He followed after Herson and took the stick from him, gripping it halfway down with one hand and pressing his forearm into the rest of the shaft. He angled the stick so that its length was pressed against the small of his back. He began walking around and swinging, fast. The sound was like a train rushing past, its wheels and engines made of crickets when the sun goes down.

At a nod from Jaka, seconded by Sabel, Tric and S'Jin and Gem and Perdite dutifully began playing a kicking game with a rag ball in case anyone wondered why the children were over here in the free hour before the final meal.

The rest of them waited for Daveedov to stop swinging. When he did, they parted the bent blades and went in.

"The reason we are here is that my sisters and I saw something in the courtyard, in the middle of the night. People came and did something to Gyre—"

"Not something," said the jumping girl.

Some of the others jumped back a little, startled. They didn't know she could speak, didn't realize her voice sounded like she was choking on a throat full of gravel. And they hadn't noticed she had come into the tall grass with them.

"Then?" Daveedov finally said to her.

"Don't sleep, don't scream," said jumping girl in a whisper, staring right at him.

"What'd she say?" asked Theson.

"She said that we saw two men kill Gyre," said Reya. "She said that they threw his body down the hatch and one went in after him. She said that the other one was at breakfast this morning, the one Chynoweth said was her cousin."

To Sabel, it seemed like no one was shocked at the idea.

No one is suddenly pining for Gyre or praying for his soul.

But in the general and heavier-feeling silence, like storm clouds that didn't break, only becoming more and more purple, like a bad bruise, Sabel knew this news about Gyre meant something for all of them. She just didn't know what.

She did know they had to figure it out fast.

"The new man. The killer. He's not her cousin," said Jaka. "You could tell from the look on her face."

"So who is he?" said Herson.

"He's dangerous. Definitely," said Reya.

"Obviously," said Theson.

"The real question is about Chynoweth. Who is she? What is she?" asked Herson.

"That's it. We don't know if she's good or bad," said Sabel. "Do you? Do any of you?"

"Maybe we should just ask her," said Daveedov.

"You mean, just ask her if she had him killed?" asked Herson.

"What if she answers yes?" asked Theson.

"What if she answers no?" asked Herson.

"She's going to answer no. Who would answer yes?" said Jaka.

"This morning, at breakfast," said Sabel. "What was that look on her face?"

"Scared," said Reya. "Scared, but trying not to look scared. Like the rest of us."

Sabel nodded at her sister, suddenly realizing that Reya knew more of what Sabel was going through than Sabel had thought. And also that Reya knew it was better for both of them, for all of them, that Reya wasn't letting on that she knew.

"So is she keeping us here, or is she being kept here along with us?" asked Jaka.

"We have to find out. We have to tell her. Maybe she doesn't even know what really happened to Gyre," said Sabel.

"But what if she does know? What if it was her idea? What if she's behind it?" asked Daveedov.

"We need to decide. Either she's with us or she's with them, whoever they are," said Jaka.

"Agreed," said Herson.

"How are we going to decide?" asked Reya.

"Let's vote," said Sabel.

Theson snorted. "Vote. Look how the world's turned out from people voting."

None of them had an answer for that.

"So what do you think we should do?" Sabel asked him.

"One of us, the strongest one, should decide," he said.

Jaka snorted. "The strongest one. Look how the world's turned out from the strongest one deciding."

Theson had no answer.

"Belief," said Sabel. "We need to believe in something to do something. We need to decide what we believe, about Chynoweth, and then we need to do something."

"Prain girl," said Jaka, nodding like something was now confirmed.

Sabel wasn't sure if this was a compliment or criticism.

She pressed on. "And I have decided I believe she's not one of them, whoever they are. She's not one of us—"

"Us?" said Theson.

"Whoever we are, she's not one of us either. But I believe she's not with the bad men, and that's enough for me. Is it enough for the rest of you?"

No one spoke. The children studied their fingers, their feet, the trees, the sky, everything and anything except each other.

"I don't believe in anything anymore. But I still believe in Sabel," said S'Jin. "So I believe what she believes."

"So do I," said Herson, looking at her.

The others nodded, or at least didn't disagree.

Sabel felt the weight of carrying this—what her little brother and the rest needed from her—but she could do it, she already had been, and knowing Herson believed in her lightened things.

"Good. So we're decided. We know the new Gyre is a bad man and we believe Chynoweth is not with the new Gyre and the other bad men," said Jaka. "So. Now. How are we going to tell her without the new bad man finding out? He eats beside her and sleeps in the room next to hers. He'll hear us."

"Inside time," said Sabel. "When she tells us those stories and asks which animal we would be. It's the only time we have her, without him."

"But, Sabel, we can't ask her in front of the others. We don't know what they might do."

"We can ask her which animal *she* would be. Or which animal Gyre had been. Or what animal the new man is. And if she understands what we're really asking . . ."

"Fine. But what happens next?" said Theson.

"Exactly. Do you really think we have enough time for telling secrets with animals during inside time?" said Jaka.

"He is a killing man," said Theri.

Verlane nodded. Jumping girl went over and stood between Verlane and Theri. Both of them moved a little closer to her.

No one said anything else.

They're taking in the warning.

Sabel could see that she had spoken with a knowingness and coldness and unchallengeable, un-taunting, un-tauntable authority she should never have had to bear.

She felt this. They all felt this. They could sense that they'd been told by little girls who knew more about the terrible world than they did. And S'Jin and Tric, always ready to push back, to prove, felt scared by the sound of their voices and grateful for their warning.

"So then what?" said Theson.

"We have to tell her tonight. We have to tell her the first chance any one of us gets. Agreed?" said Jaka.

Everyone nodded.

"So we have a plan?"

It began to rain.

Not rain rain, but nuts.

Everyone was getting hit with treenuts. It didn't hurt, but it made them look around.

In the tall grass where they stood, none of the trees was nearly close enough, and there was no wind.

With Daveedov in the lead and swinging the stick, they ran onto the playing field where the smaller children were waiting with their rag ball.

"What? Is someone coming? Was that your signal?" Jaka asked the smaller children.

"Was what our signal?" asked S'Jin.

Just then, another hail.

The treenuts were coming from somewhere inside the tall grass, aimed at all of them.

The children backed away.

"Go see who's in there!" said Theson.

"You go!" said Daveedov.

"You have the stick."

Daveedov threw the stick at Theson. It fell at his feet.

"Now you have the stick."

Another volley.

The tall grass began to sway, to bend, to break. Heads began to emerge. Dark and not ducking. Wanting to be seen.

Daveedov picked up the stick and joined the other children who had started running back to the building. Behind them, from the tall grass, came shouting.

"OBA! OBA! OBA!"

"Wait! WAIT!"

Reya sprinted to the front of the group and past the group and then she stopped and turned around and put out her hands.

"I SAID WAIT!"

Theson and Daveedov ran right past her, breathing hard. Both boys kept going, Daveedov dropping his stick when it banged into a rotting stump up along the path beside the woods that led back to the building. Sabel stopped in front of Reya.

"What? What is it, Reya?" she said.

Reya arched back up.

"What if they're trying to help us?"

"Who? THEM?" said Jaka, pointing back down the path that ended at the playing field. Everyone looked and listened, waiting to see the dark heads, hear their sounds.

"Yes. Them. They weren't throwing those treenuts to hurt us. Were any of you hurt? No. They could have pulled us in and hurt us if they wanted to. They could have jumped us in the tall grass. They didn't."

"Then what are they doing?" asked Jaka.

"Trying to get us to listen to them," said Reya.

"But what are they saying?" asked Sabel, though she already knew the answer to her question, or what it would mean to have an answer for her question. "I think Reya might be right," she continued. "I think those OBA boys might know something about what's going on."

"Or they want to drag us into the tall grass for dinner," said Perdite.

Gem took hold of Perdite's wrist and looked at their brother. Sabel looked at Perdite, wondering if she had a bad imagination or a good memory.

"Save us or eat us, we're all going to find out now," said S'Jin.

Five boys were coming up the path. They weren't rushing and they weren't chanting. They looked a little uncertain now that the children were waiting for them. The boys were wearing old shirts and pants and school ties: ragged and stained and made velvety soft and earthy brown from ground living. One of them was limping.

"Reya, take the little ones and go back to the building," said Sabel. "I'll talk to them. Reya? Are you listening?"

She wasn't. Instead, Reya was staring at the boy with the limp.

He's the one who'd smiled at her through the bus window before falling, Sabel thought. *Was he studying Reya too?*

But then Reya felt a presence beside her.

Verlane.

Verlane, studying Reya, studying the limping boy.

"Reya, why are you looking at that boy that way?"

"Quiet, Verlane! You heard Sabel. Let's go!"

"I'll stay with you," Herson said to Sabel.

"Lovebirds, even now, with the enemy approaching." muttered Tric.

"Especially now!" said Herson, beaming bright, showing a little tooth. Tric backed away. S'Jin seemed uncertain about leaving his big sister to be protected by Herson, joking at a time like this.

"It's getting close to the evening meal," Reya said to Sabel and Herson. "You need to be back before count-off. That's the only time they get upset, if they think one of us is missing. What if they ask where you are?"

"Prain girl's sister is right," said Jaka. "It's the only time they get upset. So be late. Plan to be late."

"What? Why?"

"My brother gets this voice when he gets an idea," said Gem.

"That's right. I have an idea," said Jaka.

"Listen to him when he actually has an idea," said Perdite.

"Yes. Listen to him," said Gem.

"Right," said Jaka, trying not to look so surprised and happy at his sisters' words. "So. The only thing they worry about, right, is that we are all counted. If some of us aren't there, then one of them—either Chynoweth or the new man—will come looking. Definitely one of them will come looking. The rest of you will go to dinner. Herson, you and I will find out what we can from the OBA boys and then get away from those OBA boys and be found making our way back by whoever comes to get us. If it's her, we'll tell her. If it's him, you'll tell her what we know while he's outside coming to get you."

"Fine," said Sabel. "But if it's him that comes out, what will you say about why you're late, so he doesn't—"

"I'll do whatever I can to convince him," said Herson.

"It won't be enough," said Jaka.

He called Tric and S'Jin over to him and brought them in close and asked them a question, then stepped back. Both boys raised their hands. Jaka put a finger to his lips, tapped it and pointed at S'Jin.

Suddenly the jumping girl broke away from Reya and the other small ones and ran to stand beside S'Jin and Tric.

"No. Pick me. It's the telling time."

"Pick you, over one of us?" scoffed Tric.

"You don't even know what you're being picked for," said S'Jin.

"Yes I do," she said, looking at Jaka.

"No, Jaka!" said S'Jin. "You already picked me!"

"For what?" asked his sisters in unison.

Jaka ignored them. Tric taunted the jumping girl. S'Jin brushed off his sisters and, smiling, jumped up and down in victory until Jaka lunged at him and pushed him down and stomped on his ankle three times.

"Twisted ankle. The boy needs help. Has to walk very slowly. That's why we're late," Jaka said, turning away from S'Jin, who was writhing in the brush, huffing to hold back tears and glaring at his hero.

Jumping girl went back to stand with Reya. Jaka took Tric—his own face a wrenched towel of relief and disappointment—and pushed him toward the other children. He jogged past them, picked up Daveedov's stick, and returned.

The whole while, the OBA boys were standing together lower down the path, waiting for the children to sort themselves out.

"Okay. Let's go," Jaka said to everyone else. "We were playing in the woods and S'Jin fell and hurt his ankle, and Herson and I are delayed because we are helping him get back. And just in case," Jaka said, giving Daveedov's stick to Herson.

"S'Jin, are you okay?" asked Sabel.

"Yes," he gasped. "Now go!"

Everyone except Herson and Jaka and S'Jin left.

Herson helped S'Jin up to his one foot; he couldn't put the other one down without falling over. They walked unsteadily back to the path, where S'Jin sat down on another stump. By this point, the OBA boys had come near.

"How is he going to run away now?" one of them asked.

Herson took the stick in both hands and stood in front of Jaka and S'Jin.

"You're saying we need to run away from you?" he said.

"No. Not from us."

11

THREE CHILDREN WERE MISSING FROM DINNER. Sabel told Sidian that her brother was hurt and that he was with Jaka and Herson, on the path that led to the lookout.

"Show me the way," he said, pointing Sabel ahead of him, into the dark end of the day.

Sidian was wearing Gyre's boots, which were too big for him.

She led clomping Sidian up the drive to the right of the bus, away from the building and out toward the darkening woods past dusk, when, to plan, she saw the three of them approaching, S'Jin hopping a little in between Jaka and Herson.

Sabel pointed. "There they are!"

Sidian slowed down. He stopped, waiting for them to reach him.

"Drop the stick," Sidian said from a distance.

Herson dropped the stick.

"Okay, let's go."

"Wait. You don't even want to know what happened?" said Herson, wanting to give more time to the others inside.

"He hurt his foot," said Sidian, pointing.

The children nodded.

"Okay, let's go," he repeated.

They didn't move.

"I said let's go!"

They were led back to the building in slow, foot-dragging silence.

When they were near, Sabel saw Chynoweth waiting outside the building with a couple of the other children. One of them, the warning-minded boy, ran back into the building.

"Sidian! Sidian!" Chynoweth called out.

"What? Can't you see I found them?" he called back.

"Please!" said Chynoweth, giving Sabel a quick look that told her what she needed to know. "Come quickly, Sidian! Help! The children are escaping!"

Sabel and Herson and Jaka ran behind Sidian as he sprinted the rest of the way to the building, cursing loudly at the boots that didn't fit him. Jaka and Herson ran past him, and all of them moved through the battered front door and holding hall into the building, where the children had left the dining hall and were lining the way to the inner courtyard, pointing and looking scared. Sabel watched Sidian follow their pointing into the lamp-lit courtyard, where Jaka had joined Daveedov in holding the wooden cover of the well and jumping girl was balanced on top of the open hole.

She was about to escape!

Other children were lining the way to the well. They looked

like they were waiting to go down next.

"DON'T!" Sidian screamed, stopping.

The little girl dropped down the hole.

"NO!"

"Sidian! She's the one! She's the one! Get her!" said Chynoweth, suddenly at his side.

Sidian charged at the well and the children stepped back as he approached, including the boys still holding the well cover.

Going full tilt into the gloaming in boots too big for him, he didn't see the children near the well stick their legs out to trip him. He fell hard.

The two boys holding the well cover stepped over and dropped it on his head.

Picking it up, they dropped it on his head a second time.

They did this a third time.

The sound was like a hard fruit dropped from a high distance.

Then the sound was like a plate of small fried birds for breakfast.

Then the sound was like nothing other than what it was.

A human life, destroyed.

They did this a fourth time.

Now it was like something else altogether.

Sabel stared at the boys' faces. Their bulging wet eyes, their set mouths: they looked like they could do this for the rest of their lives.

Chynoweth told them to stop.

Jaka and Daveedov dropped the lid immediately, each of them sobbing, while it banged down against the stones.

Seeing the scene before her, knowing what had just happened, not knowing what was going to happen next, Sabel felt as if an unseen giant had just flipped a coin to determine the rest of their lives. In the dark, she couldn't tell which side was up.

Chynoweth told the older children to gather the younger children and for everyone to go into the library and wait there. They went. No one thought to tell the jumping girl she could come back out from her perch inside the well, the one she had found on the day they arrived.

But this wasn't the first time in her raked and blown-around, cindering life that jumping girl had gone down into a well, either to hide or escape.

Sabel finally remembered and went to get her, by which point she had already climbed out and was standing beside Sidian's body.

Sabel held out a hand, she took it and the two of them ran to Reya and the other sisters, who had also come back for jumping girl and were waiting in the threshold to the courtyard.

They hugged and kept her close.

Meanwhile, Chynoweth had gone back to the dining hall. She found the cook in the back, washing bits of rice and beans and cabbage off the meal trays, as usual.

Head down, staring at the reddish metal-finned water.

But he must have heard something, she thought.

"Are you going back down the mountain now?" asked Chynoweth.

"Yes. I have to leave soon," he said, not looking up.

"And?"

He kept washing.

"I have to leave soon. It's only my wife and daughter down there. They cannot prepare the meal for the group by themselves."

"They are keeping my father too. Do you know the man I mean?"

Not looking up. Still washing.

"Are you going to tell them?" she asked.

He stopped the water and pulled up a stack of trays, lifting them up and down to drain them, then left them to the side of the sink and did it a second and then a third time.

He did the same with fistfuls of spoons.

He dried his hands on his pants and walked toward the door at the back of the kitchen. Chynoweth followed him and then slipped in front, blocking his way.

"Are you going to tell them?" she asked.

The old man sighed.

"Girl, are you also going to take me by the wrist and put your love of ghee against my love?"

She winced and flamed.

"Ghee? I don't love ghee. I love my father. I just want to get out of here with him."

"Really? That's all? You don't care at all about anyone else? About these children? Then why don't you just do what they tell you? Why did you just—"

He caught his breath, like he was about to fall off a sudden ledge.

He looked scared.

But for the first time, he looked directly at her, his eyes the feel and colour of riverstones: blue and veined and faded to lined and grey.

Riverstone: old and forgotten among so many others, yes, but still wet, still hard.

"What will happen, uncle, if you tell them?" she asked. "Will they let you and yours go and take me instead? What will they do to me? What will they do to my father? What will they do to these children? I believed what the children told me about him. That's why we did it."

"You believed what children said, girl. You put your life at risk. You put others' lives at risk because you believed what children said. These children. These safe and cared for children, even here, even now, so much safer and cared for than any other children. You are risking everything, because of them? Do you think they would do the same for you, for yours, when their papas come in their bullet-car motorcades?"

"I believed what the children told me about him."

"Why? This could hurt you. It could hurt your father. Others. Why?"

"Because they needed me to believe them. Because they took the risk first, in telling me, in believing that I would believe them and I would help them. And they were right."

He nodded, first to himself and then to her.

"I'll come back for the morning meal. And tomorrow night, I will return for the evening meal. All as usual. Don't worry about his group. None of them asks me anything about my coming and going here. None of them asks me anything. They only ask for more food and when is my daughter going to stop hiding in the kitchen and start coming to the table."

Chynoweth nodded.

He lingered.

His eyes dried. But they turned harder.

"The answer is never. Never while I'm living."

He left.

Chynoweth caught the door before it closed and watched him get into his small, wood-slatted truck. He turned it around much faster than seemed possible in the stone-walled side slot and drove toward the main road, getting out and trotting off into the near woods to do whatever had to be done for the three barriers to lower so he could drive down the mountain.

Chynoweth closed the back door and left the kitchen. She walked through the dining hall and looked, then looked away, from the moon-lit inner courtyard—the body by the well.

She entered the library, which was lit by foggy-glassed orbs suspended from the raftered ceiling. The children looked like they were studying, whether the spines of books written in different languages, or the many stages of the history of this particular room's spiderwebs, or the whorling knots and grey-black crevices in the floor, or their overgrown fingernails, or just their shoes. Whatever it took to not look at anyone else, ask or be asked about what had just happened, about what might happen next.

12

"CHILDREN," CHYNOWETH SAID. "Children, look at me, please."

Two did not. The rest looked up for a moment, their faces showing everything, and then back they went to the spines of books and spiderwebs and fingernails and dirty shoes.

The two who didn't look up were Jaka and Daveedov. They didn't feel like children, just then. They were staring at their hands. From where she was standing, Sabel could see their purpling fat worm-shaped welts that had formed while gripping the lid of the well and slamming it down again and again.

Again and again and again and again.

Sabel's head throbbed. *Do they feel bad about what they just did? Or good?*

"Everyone, I said look at me, please."

Chynoweth waited.

Not everyone looked.

"I said look at me!"

They all looked.

Now more softly, "Children, we are all safer because of what we just did."

She let that settle in.

It didn't seem to settle in.

The air in the library, already heavy, began to feel closer, the breathing tighter.

The warning-minded boy popped up to show Chynoweth that he was shaking his head in disagreement with what she had just said.

The rest of the children were glaring at each other. Whatever was going on inside of them, Sabel knew they didn't have time for this. She caught Chynoweth's gaze and nodded to encourage her to keep going.

"We are all safer because of what we just did," she repeated, "but we are not safe for very long."

"Because of what we just did," said Theson.

Jaka and Daveedov looked up from their welted hands.

They glared at him.

"*We?*" Jaka asked. "Where were you? You definitely weren't in the courtyard. And I knew you weren't going to do it. That's why I ran ahead when he was coming."

"We were already not safe, which is why we did what we just did," Sabel said.

"And we remain not safe. Correct, Chynoweth?" said Herson.

She nodded.

"But that's not right! That wasn't the plan!" said another girl. "We were sent here by our parents to be kept safe. And you are saying we are not safe in this place."

"Bad men came and took over from the people who used to be here. Then men even worse than them sent Sidian here," said Chynoweth.

"Were you one of them?" asked the girl who had asked Gyre about the colour of money on the first day.

"Are you one of them?" asked the boy who'd told the children the story of his mother and her workpartydress.

"No," said Chynoweth.

"Why should we believe you?" asked the girl who had heard that story and still believed she had the worst story of all.

"They took my father. The bad men did. They took him to make me take care of all of you. To pretend Gyre was my brother while he watched us. And then when a new group of bad men came, they sent one of them here to get rid of Gyre."

"And we got rid of him," said S'Jin, not with pride but not with shame either.

"Why would our parents send us away from bad men to a place full of bad men!" sobbed another child.

"They didn't know this when they sent you here," said Chynoweth. "They thought they were sending you here to be safe, or at least safer from your part of the falling-down world."

"As if it's going to be safe again when we go back," the same child sobbed.

"Ghee," said S'Jin matter of factly.

"He means that this is expensive, but getting somewhere else is also expensive," said Tric. "So probably the parents are all taking these ten days to get enough ghee to take us somewhere safer than home and safer than this place."

S'Jin nodded in agreement.

"Chynoweth, why do you think the world is the way it is right now? Why is the world falling down?" asked the sobbing girl, who stopped crying just long enough to ask her question.

Other children made upset noises in agreement.

Sabel sent Reya across the room, Verlane and Theri joining, to comfort the sobbing girl and make sure she didn't ask any more questions. Then Sabel nodded at Chynoweth to continue.

Because even if she wasn't sobbing or making upset noises in agreement, Sabel had the same question.

Why was the world as it was?

"There are people in this world who have a lot less than people like me have," said Chynoweth. "And there are people in this world who have a lot more than people like you have. And the people who have less than me decided it was time to take from the people who have more than you."

"And we're caught in the middle," said Sabel.

"So, are they going to take us?" asked the boy with the mother in the workpartydress.

Chynoweth said nothing. Her only idea had been to drive the bus somewhere else, but she didn't know how to drive, or if anyone else did, or even how to lower the little barriers that blocked the roadway. And she knew the cook wouldn't drive them and risk his own wife and daughter. Chynoweth said nothing.

Sabel, studying Chynoweth and feeling a dangerous space opening between questions and answers in the library, looked at Herson, hoping he'd learned something from the OBA boys.

"We can go up the road," he said, "or we can go into the positive woods."

"The positive woods?"

"It's the forest all around us," said Herson.

"Why is it called positive?"

"It's what they call it," said S'Jin.

"Who's they? The bad men?"

S'Jin shook his head.

"Who's they?" asked another of the children. "What's the positive woods?"

"Listen to S'Jin, everyone," said Jaka, looking up. "He knows what's next."

But this was no time for praise.

"I don't know what's next," S'Jin said. "Maybe I have an idea from what I heard Jaka and Herson talking about with the OBA boys."

"OBA boys?" asked the warning-minded boy.

"They are children who were sent to this same place before it was taken over," said Herson. "And back then, when the boat returned, they weren't on the list to go back."

"What list?"

"They didn't say. Probably the same kind of list we were all on when we were brought here. The OBA boys only said that when the boat came back, they were told that their parents didn't send for them to return, and they weren't allowed to stay in the school anymore, so they went into the woods and lived there instead."

"OBA means Old Boys Association," said Sabel.

Many of the children nodded at a term they had heard from fathers, uncles, grandfathers.

Now they'll all be wondering if their parents will have sent for them when the boat comes back, Sabel thought, not wondering this about Amma and Appa.

Of course they will.

Of course any parent would.

"Those boys live in the woods? How? How long?" said Theson.

"I don't know how long. They found some abandoned houses in the woods, and that's where they've stayed."

"What happened to the people who used to live in the houses?" asked the warning-minded boy.

"The sickness," Sabel continued.

"Is that why it's called the positive woods?" said the boy. "I don't want to go there."

"We won't," said Chynoweth.

"I have a question for you then," said Theson, looking directly at Chynoweth.

"Ask."

"You say we can't stay here. You say we can't move into the woods, whatever they're called. So where do you say we should go?"

Chynoweth ignored his question. She turned to Jaka and Herson and whispered, "Something will have to be done with the body after we leave the library. And someone needs to keep watch in the night."

"NO WHISPERING! No secrets! We all did this. We all should hear what you are saying," said an older girl.

"Or were you just planning where some of you are going next? Are you going to leave the rest of us here?" asked another.

"We have to think that, if you're whispering secrets," said the first girl. "Or tell us what we are going to do now."

Chynoweth didn't say anything.

She didn't know.

Her face went slack and her body relaxed, like a taut rope tied tightly, when suddenly the knot begins to give.

Theson saw and stood up. A few of the others also saw. He noticed that too.

"You don't know what to do, do you!" Theson scoffed, pointing across the crowded library at Chynoweth. "You just made us kill that man—and I don't care that we did what we just did to that killing man, I already knew it had to be done—but you don't know what we should do next. And we're all in this place, listening to you tell us you don't know what to do now. So why are you still in charge? Who are you, even? Who put you in charge? Why should we do anything more for you?"

"For me? For me?" Chynoweth stalked into the middle of the room, her green eyes popping and going dark as if blood was filling behind them. Everyone shrank back, except Theson, who held his ground, legs twitching. "NO! Why should I do anything more for any of you?" she asked.

Theri raised her hand. Verlane pulled it down. They exchanged words quietly and vehemently. Then Verlane nodded and raised her hand.

"What is it?" Chynoweth said flatly.

"You're in charge," said Verlane. "We listen to you. That's why."

"That's why what?" asked Chynoweth, looking confused.

Verlane looked confused too.

"You just asked why you should do anything more for any of us, didn't you?"

Chynoweth sighed. "I'm just a bookseller's daughter and this island isn't my home. I was brought here. My brother is dead. My mother is dead. They have my father. I have tried, children. I have tried and tried. But . . ." She fell silent.

"We will leave here tomorrow," Sabel said with suddenness and strength. "Does everyone agree?"

"I do," said Herson. "There is a place we can go. Higher up the mountain."

"Yes. We should go up," said S'Jin.

"The OBA boys told us about this place," said Herson.

"And we believe them," said S'Jin.

"Can we walk there, right up the main road?" asked Chynoweth.

"Yes," he said.

Most of the other children were nodding by now. Chynoweth nodded too. "Then we leave in the morning," she said.

"What kind of place is it, up the mountain?" Theson asked. "Why believe the OBA boys? What makes it safer? Why should we believe any of you? Because you're the ones in charge?"

He looked around the library for children who agreed with him. There were a few.

"Do you want to be in charge?" Jaka asked him. "Yes or no?"

"He doesn't know—"

"Yes he does! He knows exactly what he is doing," said Jaka, cutting off Herson. "Since we got here, he has been pushing and pushing and pushing about everything, but not doing anything himself. Look at my hands, everyone. See these marks? Now look at Daveedov's."

Daveedov held out his hands.

"Same," he said.

"Now what about yours, Theson?" asked Jaka. "You weren't even in the courtyard. We. We. There is no you in our we, okay? So now it's time to change that. Right now, in front of us all, take charge, mega man, or stop this and join. What's it going to be?"

Theson made straight for Jaka, who planted his feet, ready. Herson made to get in between them but before he could, Theson swerved toward the library door and left.

No one followed him. Not even Herson.

"We leave in the morning," said Sabel. "We walk up the mountain road. We are going to a safe place. At least, a safer place than this."

13

THE NEXT MORNING, before the cook came with the first meal, they walked out of the building onto the main road. While only a few of the older children had been chosen to keep watch, none of them had slept. The air was cold, the sun was rising, and it was raining. They didn't know who or what was going to be waiting for them up the road. They were all very much awake.

Sabel was in front and Chynoweth was at the back. The children crowded together in between. S'Jin hung from Jaka's shoulders.

Not all the children were walking up the road, Sabel noticed. Two were missing.

She turned and saw Herson, well behind the group but moving fast to join it, his face furious and resolved and streaked with more than rain.

As much as she wanted to walk beside him, Sabel let him be; he looked like he needed to walk alone for a while along the pitted and cracked road.

Past Herson, Sabel saw one person standing by himself at the turn to the main road, resting his hand on one of the little stone pillars to look at ease with being left by himself, but failing to look at ease.

Theson.

Why didn't he want to go with the rest of them? Sabel wondered. *Was his pride that wounded by what had happened in the library the night before? Was more pride really the cure?*

Sabel turned back and walked past everyone, including Chynoweth. Jumping girl noticed and followed, taking her by the arm.

"No. Not you," she told Sabel. "I will make him come with us."

Jumping girl didn't wait for an answer.

She drew close to Theson and they spoke briefly. Theson shook his head. He stepped back and crossed his arms and scoffed.

She said something else. He shook his head more slowly this time.

She waited.

She waited.

Suddenly, Theson dashed past her and kept going until he was in the middle of the other children, his head down.

Sabel linked up with jumping girl returning to the group. Before she could ask, jumping girl said, "I told him to come with us."

"And so he came? That's all?"

"I asked him if he knew how to hold on to the notches inside the well for when he would be thrown into it."

"You said the bad men are going to catch him and throw him down the well?"

"No. I told him that if he didn't come with us, we would catch him and throw him down the well."

Jumping girl moved past Sabel, returning to her place beside Verlane and Theri.

The way she'd said it, in that scraped voice, Sabel thought, *was enough to convince Theson.*

She believed her too.

And so, together they went up the road in the cold bright wet, now with Herson in front and by himself. There was no talking among them, no sound other than the patter of pinning rain. They were prepared, and terrified, to hear a vehicle approaching from far off. Only then would they do what they didn't want to otherwise: go into the woods, the positive woods, where, if they looked closely, they would see several boys in ragged school uniforms walking beside them, in front of them, and behind. The OBA boys were making sure the children made it up the mountain. And they were ready to pull them into the woods if anyone tried to stop them.

But the children didn't look closely enough. They were too ragged from little to no sleep, wet eyed and squinting in rain and sudden sunlight, and looking only at what was immediately ahead, and not beside them.

After a time that felt very long to some of them, if sudden to others, they reached a bend in the road.

"Herson, stop! Look!" Sabel called ahead.

He turned around and his angry, stomped-feeling heart flipped and floated. Not from seeing Sabel but from seeing

Theson, walking in the middle of the group. Or at least he saw the familiar top of Theson's dark, short-haired head. Theson was looking down. The rest of them were looking right at Herson.

No, they weren't looking at him. They were looking past him.

"No! Not at us! Turn around and look!" said Sabel.

Herson turned and looked ahead.

The road led right into a tiny piazza with an open space surrounded by little stalls and shops and restaurants. All the buildings were made of sandy orange stone.

A fountain filled the middle of the square, its centre a greened shaft of metal with green metal fish bending and leaping up and away, but stuck there.

The fountain was empty.

The square was empty.

The stalls and shops and restaurants were boarded up or boarded up and busted through long ago.

The rain stopped.

Their clothes were damp.

Sabel's ears were wringing with listening for some kind of signal, whether of danger or safety.

There was nothing. No signal.

The far side of the square ended at a high and broad wall of the same stone. Sabel noticed that the top of the wall looked different than everywhere else in the square. It had thin lines of green, of deep green vines.

Living things.

These vines were running from where to where? she wondered.

Grown and kept by whom?

The vines didn't extend far down the wall, which had a massive closed gate set into it. The gate itself had a small simple door in one corner.

The door began to open.

14

SABEL SAW A ROUNDISH MAN step out of the door. He was wearing an untucked white shirt and very dirty pants. But dirty with soil, not blood.

Everyone stepped back and moved closer together.

They studied this man, studying them.

This was the first non-tarp-living person they'd seen in a long while who still had long hair.

Sabel remembered the sickness, something none of them had thought about since their first days of coming here, jabbed and shaved.

He didn't smile and beckon, like they were maybe hoping.

He didn't smile and come for them, like they were fearing.

He stared at them for what felt like an eternity, pulling the bottom of his chin.

"Where are you from?" he called across the town square.

But they were from all sorts of places.

"Are you all staying at the Away School?"

"Yes we are," said Sabel.

"Are there any more of you, down the mountain?"

"No. It's just us, and we're here now," said Chynoweth, stepping in front. "Can you let us in?"

"We let people come in here when they have nowhere else to go. We don't turn anyone away. We have no weapons. We offer no lessons. We only ask that people help where they can, and help each other, and take nothing unless they give something too. Again, we have no weapons. We have no lessons. And you are a lot of little strangers, suddenly, and no word was sent before you arrived. Would you let in a group of strangers like you?"

"Yes," said Sabel.

"And why is that?" he asked her.

"Because we are not strangers like you mean strangers. We are children who were sent to this island, to the, the . . ."

"Away School," her sisters around her said softly.

"Away School, to be kept safe, but we are not safe. Because strangers came after us, and we had to get away," said Sabel. She realized what the letters on the dining hall spelled, even if by now you could only make out YOOL.

"We have nowhere else to go, okay? We were told to come here," said Jaka, coming forward. "So will you let us in, like you say you do, or do we have to go back to the other people? The real strangers. The bad men."

"Where are these real strangers right now? These bad men? Will they follow you here?" asked the long-haired man.

"No," said Chynoweth.

"How can you know this?" he asked.

"The way we made sure they don't know . . . is why we have to come here now," said Daveedov.

His voice strained when he said this. The children around him closed in. He wiped his eyes.

The man bit his lip.

Who needed details, hearing a voice like that?

"Who told you to come here?" the man said.

"OBA!" S'Jin called out from Jaka's back.

"The old schoolboys from the positive woods?"

"OBA!" Tric called out, standing beside Jaka.

Sabel and others nodded.

"Are they okay? The boys, I mean," the man asked.

"We spoke to them," said Reya.

"And?" the man said.

"They are okay," said Sabel.

"They're probably watching us all right now, from somewhere close," he said, louder.

Everyone looked around and waited, squinting and shivering and ears straining in the cold brightness of the silent square.

Nothing.

"Well, they know they can also come inside, whenever they want," he called out. "As for the rest of you, come inside. There isn't enough food, but there never has been enough food. And everyone is fed. We're all still here. My name is Breuther."

They crossed the town square.

But then Breuther turned at someone speaking to him from inside the doorway. He nodded.

"Wait. WAIT!" he said to them.

They stopped.

"You should know what it means that we let everyone in here who has nowhere else to go."

"We heard what you said about food and shelter," said Chynoweth.

"And about weapons and lessons," said Sabel.

"No. Not that. We let everyone in. But they are from this island. They are not strangers."

"We know what that means too, and that's why we have come to you," she said.

"Yes. But also, they are not Away School people, not people like you, not like your parents. *Now* do you know what that means?"

Chynoweth didn't.

No one else did either.

"They don't have short hair showing their necks, their jab berry bruises. Now do you understand?" he asked. "The sickness. It means there are people in here with the sickness. They are staying in tents on one of our fields, because there's no one to watch them in the huts where sickness people used to be sent on this island."

Herson stepped forward. "Our jabs protect us, so we won't get the sickness by going inside."

"And we're not sugar diamonds, okay? We're not! If you knew what's been going on at this so-called school . . ." called out Perdite.

"We've lived in prisons that were safer!" said Gem.

"Okay, okay, this isn't about us," said Jaka, turning toward the girls.

They scowled and batted away his quieting hands. Meanwhile, the other children were nodding in agreement with them.

They must be feeling like these past few days have crushed them into something less sweet than a sugar diamond, Sabel thought. They had become something harder and sharper, capable of reflecting less brilliant light, and this was a good thing: they had found themselves in a time and place where brightness changed from being the key to everything to being a lock on themselves, a danger. Getting sick, not getting sick, jabbed or not jabbed, mothers worrying or not worrying: luxury goods when you lived with killing men.

"Sabel," Reya said, pointing at Breuther, who was motioning for them to approach.

Passing through the small door, they entered a wide grassy space. Some of them immediately looked behind them, just in case. But no one was following. Only the door, shutting.

They breathed in cold air and their eyes moved from the shut door to the greenery growing up the inside of the wall—vines and stalks, potted in ginger-coloured wooden boxes. This was the first aliveness they had seen since coming to the island. But they turned around quickly at the smell cutting through the cold.

Where was it coming from, that smell?

Was it what they thought it was?

They followed Breuther down a laneway made of chipped and broken stones, stones that weren't chipped and broken by heavy vehicles and hot falling metal. They were chipped and broken by many lifetimes of weather, footfall, hoof and wheel. So too the laneway itself was lined with grand stone bases on which stood tributes to great ones, whether heroes or saints, monsters or gods. Sabel couldn't tell, because so much of each statue had long since fallen away. Again though, what was missing, you could tell, wasn't because of angry hammers or heaving ropes, but from time and weather, by the world itself. The laneway led to a larger building on a treeless rise, which for its roof had two great domes. Beyond that, dark blue and darker blue: the sky and the sea.

They kept walking.

To one side of the laneway were several buildings made of the same stone as the Away School, and also what looked like outdoor rooms. These were separated from each other by see-through shelves full of dull-coloured pots and dishes. Some of the rooms had sinks and ovens made of stacked bricks. Smoke was rising.

This is where it was coming from.

It was a good smoke.

People were preparing food—baking bread, loaves and loaves and loaves—in the outdoor rooms. Some looked up from their work. Of those, a few smiled. A few nodded. One or two shook their heads. Those who smiled called words across worktables to those who had shaken their heads, who then nodded in agreement with whatever had been said and then weakly, apologetically, smiled at Sabel. All of them went back to their work.

Farther along, in another outside room, a big black pot sat on a cinderblock square. Red orange flames waved against the bottom of the pot. Two people were stirring whatever was inside.

Seeing the children, one of the cooks went to a shelf and took out clay cups and set these on the table beside the pot, where many such cups waited already.

Had all the island's people come here when this place joined the rest of the falling-down world? Sabel wondered.

On the other side of the wide grassy space was an expanse of tents, some made of canvas. Many people milled about—their cheeks like old firewood and hair like frayed rope, their bodies like sickles and commas and shepherd's crooks. Also children, lots of them, running and playing barefoot until they saw the new people, the new children, and stopped and stared, some of them craning around the monument bases lining the pathway.

These children chinned at the new children, who stopped walking and pretended to study their shoes.

"You should go talk to them for us," Sabel heard Theson say to Herson.

"Why him? Because he's braver than you?" asked Tric.

"No. That's not, I'm not trying to . . ."

"Then why? Because I'm one of them instead of one of you?" said Herson.

"Well, yes. You're one of us, but out of all of us, you're most like one of them," said Theson.

Herson scowled.

Theson pursed his lips. He looked like he wanted to say something else. For the first time, he didn't look like a lemon-sucking princeling.

What did he look like instead?

Like someone who, for the first time in his life, was trying, *really* trying, to be someone other than everything in his life had made him into being.

But no one was noticing.

Fresh bread mattered more than a fresh chance.

After how he'd behaved already, fresh bread or no fresh bread, it seemed no one wanted to hear what Theson was trying to say.

Soon he was standing there by himself, stared at by the tent children.

The rest of the children were following Breuther toward the fresh bread and hot soup.

One returned for him.

Again.

"Don't stay there. Come with us," said jumping girl.

But unlike the last time, her voice wasn't the threat of a rusty hammer thrown right at him. Someone who had been left behind too many times wasn't going to leave anyone behind, not even this one.

He followed her.

Meanwhile, the tent people told their children to stop staring.

They went back to running and playing. But some still stared at the new ones.

"What is this place? Excuse me, Brother. What is this place?" asked Sabel.

Breuther stopped and turned.

"Breuther. *Breuther*. My name is Breuther."

"But aren't you prain people?" asked Perdite.

"What's prain people?" asked Breuther.

"She means, what you're doing here, whatever it is," said Jaka. "You're not doing it for ghee, you're doing it for God, right?"

"Why do you think so?"

"Because you look like prain people, you sound like prain people, you act like prain people," said Gem.

"And what do you think of prain people?" asked Breuther.

"Some of us are prain people! The sister-girls. Where are they? They can show you how they hold hands before eating," called Perdite.

Theri tugged at Sabel.

"What if that man decides we are so like him that we have to stay here and never go home to Appa and Amma?" she asked. "Going home to Amma and Appa is still happening, isn't it? Yes or no?"

Sabel smiled and nodded.

Not to answer her question, but to say she had the same question.

Yes or no?

Like her sisters, her brother, and all the other children, Sabel had these two answers sitting in her heart and mind.

"Whoever you are, whatever you do, thank you for letting us come in here. But what is this place?" said Chynoweth.

"What is it now, you mean? I already told you," said Breuther.

"Yes. I know it is a place of safety for people who have nowhere to go. That's what you told us outside the wall and that's why we are here. But these statues, that building at the end of the path, with domes . . ."

"It's called a specolave. For looking at the stars. How or why, I don't know. Only that it's been done at this place for a very long time. If you want to know more, you'd have to ask Magnificent Rector."

"When can we meet Magnificent Rector?" asked Perdite.

"You can't."

"Is he too important for us?" asked Gem.

"No. Well, yes, yes he is. But that's not why you can't meet him."

"Then why? The sickness?" asked Jaka.

Breuther nodded.

Everyone was quiet.

"Aren't you hungry?" he said.

They had left the Away School that morning without breakfast. And that first smell of fresh bread had stayed with them.

The children moved quickly to where the food was being given out.

Only Chynoweth remained. "Do you want me to tell you what really brought us here?" she asked Breuther.

"What difference will it make? You're already here. Also, I don't think any of you are from this island, are you."

"No. Why?"

"It's not the first time this has happened."

"What has happened?"

"The sickness. The latest smashings and crashings. All of it sending everyone the way all have gone and will go. Maybe this is worse than other times. Maybe. But this place has been here a very long time. It was once the summer palace of the island king, as it was for his fathers before him—they are the statues. He fell, and so did the statues, and by the time the fighting had finished, the weather had changed and none of the new mega men wanted to rebuild a ruin in the snow."

"A ruin in the snow?" Chynoweth repeated.

"Yes. One of the only buildings that's still standing from that time is the specolave."

"Why do you have a specolave?"

"There was once a royal astronomer. His job was to stare at the sky and look for the shape of the island king in the stars, the shape of his enemies, and nothing other than that. When the first Magnificent Rector came with his people and saw how much more could be seen of the stars, the work began. And so the other buildings were built or rebuilt, and the sky was studied, and we got on with things—some of us studied the skies and some of us, like me, took care of everything on the ground. We were left alone and left others alone, but from parents down to children, children to their children, the islandborn people, not from elsewhere—everyone knew this as a place they could come when they needed to. Including all of you."

Breuther nodded at her and then at the children.

Sabel followed his gaze and looked over at the others, standing near the tables of food, tearing through fresh bread and sipping from bowls of hot soup. Some were hopping around after burning their tongues. Others were pointing at them, laughing. The children were laughing. All of them, finally, had a little time to be children.

"Thank you, for taking us in," Chynoweth said.

He nodded.

"People came here not just when it was needed. Even people like yours. In the better times, the parents of Away School children would come here and buy our bread and the plates we make and ask about any nice places to eat nearby, and yacht and jet wives would tell us they wanted simpler lives and they'd buy our honey and honey candles while their husbands asked how much to buy the whole place."

He laughed.

"The better times?" asked Chynoweth.

"Maybe not so better times."

"Those are not my people."

"I know. But they are probably the people of the children you're watching, aren't they? So this is your job then? To watch these children, keep them safe? But what happened? Something went wrong at the Away School, and the children didn't run into the positive woods like the OBA boys. Instead you brought them here because this is your job, to watch them, to keep them, yes?"

"No," said Chynoweth.

"No?"

"It's not my job."

"Then?"

"It had to be done."

But she knew that at some point Sidian's men would go to the school. Finding no one there, they'd begin to look for them. Eventually they would find this place. What would they do to all these people in here?

Maybe nothing, if the one they sought, the treasure child, was sent out to the other side of the wall.

Which one is it? she wondered.

"What? What is it?" said Breuther, seeing the worried look on Chynoweth's face.

"Bad men have my father. They're holding him there to force me into taking care of these children."

"Where are they?" asked Breuther.

But she didn't answer him. She didn't need to.

Everyone inside the wall heard and smelled something coming from outside the wall.

Engines.

Engine smoke.

They were here.

They had found them.

They had come for them.

For one of them.

Which one?

15

"DID YOU TELL THEM WE WERE HERE?" Chynoweth asked.

"No. Shall I ask you the same question?" said Breuther.

"We didn't tell them we were coming here. We didn't even know what this place was. We didn't think they would follow us."

"But . . ." Breuther was nodding, chewing on his lip and the hair around it. "But you do know who it is. Who's out there. What they want."

"I have an idea, yes."

"An idea."

Breuther was still nodding, trying to do nothing other than nod. This was a place where you accepted anyone who came, no questions asked. Right now, from the sounds and smells of those engines outside the wall, he had the very strong sense that these weren't people to be let inside.

"Whoever they are, they have come here to get all of you," he said.

"No. Not all of us. Just—"

Breuther held up his hand.

"Listen to me," Chynoweth said. "They want to—"

But he turned and began walking away.

Everyone was watching him go.

When he passed through the door in the wall, the engines stopped. The smoke lingered.

Inside, they couldn't hear anything.

Anything at all.

So they began staring instead.

The people who had been living here already were staring at Chynoweth and the Away School children, all of them still holding the cups of soup and crusts of bread they'd been given.

These people are thinking that food could have been kept for themselves, Sabel thought. *Or at least given to strangers who didn't bring worse strangers with them.*

Meanwhile, Chynoweth and the children were staring at the ground, avoiding those stares from the others. They had moved in close to each other. But none of the islandborn staring people made a move, or muttered anything that could be heard across the stone path dividing them.

Everyone waited for Breuther to return.

After only a few minutes, he walked in through the door in the wall.

Immediately everyone waited to hear the engines start again, to know that whoever they were, whyever they had come, Breuther had spoken and now they were leaving.

But the engines didn't start again.

Breuther walked partway toward Chynoweth and the children and motioned to them to approach.

For Sabel and the others, this was a long and very watched walk.

"I'm supposed to say two things to all of you," he said.

"Okay," Chynoweth said.

"First, the boat is here."

"Okay. I thought it was supposed to come tomorrow."

"So you do know what that means? That the boat has come? You believe them? You're all leaving?"

"Yes. No."

"Which one?"

"Not all of us are leaving."

"Then who's the boat for? Why did they tell me to tell you that?"

"The boat's not for me. It's for the children. I don't have anywhere else to go. But never mind. What's the second thing they said to say to me?"

"They brought out an old man from one of their vehicles. He said, I think it goes like, 'Kataba kataba kataba ka'?"

Chynoweth fell, crying.

The other children moved closer.

"Is it about us?" asked the warning-minded boy.

"Is it about your brother? Is Gyre okay?" asked a little one.

Verlane glared at the child who clearly still had no idea what was happening.

"They have my father," Chynoweth said.

"And they want you to trade him for us, right?" said S'Jin.

"No. It's not that," she said. "They held him in their camp to make me watch all of you."

"Until this?" asked Sabel.

Chynoweth nodded.

"But what is this? What's going on?" asked Jaka. "Who's outside the wall?"

"Step back. Children, step back. Let her be for a moment. I'm sure she'll answer your questions. Step back, children," said Breuther.

They stepped back.

All but one of the children. Jumping girl came and stood beside Chynoweth, catching her wrist in one hand and holding it until Chynoweth stood up.

The people already living inside the wall began to approach, but Breuther motioned to them to stop. They didn't move away, but they didn't come any closer either.

"Chynoweth, please tell us what is happening," said Sabel.

"Children, I am sorry to tell you, but I don't really know what is happening."

"Liar," muttered the girl who still believed she had the worst story of them all.

Chynoweth suddenly stood straighter. Her green eyes were now dry, even bright. She hadn't said much to them about what she'd known all along, but she had never lied. This was like a crack of light under a barred door. It was light enough for her sights.

"No. I'm not a liar. I'm not. Children, I was never anything, until suddenly I was, until I had to be someone for others—for my father, and for all of you. And whatever I am, whatever I'm going to become or who you think I am or you someday may remember me as, I am not a liar. I'm a bookseller's daughter. I'm not a teacher or part of the Away School. I never said I was. Just before you were brought here, I was brought here by a group of men that included Gyre, who wasn't my brother. They held my father in their camp and told me to watch over you, as if I worked at the Away School. Sidian, who wasn't my cousin just like Gyre wasn't my brother, was part of a new group that took over from Gyre's group. Gyre wasn't a good man. He was . . . only, not a bad man. Sidian was a killing man. And it seems Sidian's men have found us."

"And they say the boat has arrived to take you back to your parents," Breuther said.

"How can we know that the boat has arrived to take us back?" asked Jaka.

"The specolave," said Breuther.

"The what?" said Jaka.

Gem and Perdite pointed at the domed building a distance away from them, on a rise.

"At the end of the red metal staircase in the corner of the main hall—not the stone stairway that you'll see first, but the red metal staircase—there is a door. The door leads to the roof. You can walk around the roof. Standing near the dome on the left, you can see the harbour. You'll be able to see whether the boat has come."

Jumping girl let go of Chynoweth's wrist and ran toward the specolave. So did Herson. The rest of them watched.

"Sabel, go," said Reya.

"You're the faster runner," said Sabel. "And anyway Herson is already going."

"Exactly," said Reya.

"Exactly what?"

Reya cocked her head.

"What?" said Sabel.

"What if this is it?" asked Reya.

"Why?"

"*Herson*. What if this is the only chance you'll ever have?"

"Chance for what? Oh. Oh. *Now?*"

"No, at the next name-day party at the Patriot's Club, drinking glasses of bloomflower before the last dance. Yes, now! Go!"

Sabel ran after him.

Jumping girl was first to return.

"And?" said Breuther.

"The boat's there," she said.

"She's right. And two others. Smaller ones," said Herson, catching up, flushed.

"Yes," Sabel nodded, also flushed.

"Okay. So now what? We all leave now?" said Jaka.

"No, children. No," said Chynoweth.

"Then?"

"She *is* going to trade us for her father!" said the warning-minded boy.

"No. Children, listen to me. This is what I know. One of you is not going to that boat."

"How long have you known this?" asked Theson.

"Why didn't you tell us earlier?" asked Herson.

"Which one of us, Chynoweth?" asked Theri.

The little one asked with such an open face, a trusting, unknowing, open face, Chynoweth had to look away.

But in this moment, this suddenly late-feeling moment, they all had such faces. Even the scowls on the older children's faces failed to hold.

Big eyes, plain brows, still mouths. They were all waiting to be told, no, it's not you, you're safe.

Or, no, you're not safe. It's you they've come for.

"I don't know which one of you it is," said Chynoweth. "I was never told. I don't even know if Gyre's group or Sidian's group knows. What I know is that someone is coming for one of you, and these groups of men have been fighting to hold onto all of you so they can give one of you over."

"Some kind of mega man, probably," said Jaka.

"Mega-ghee," said Tric.

Jaka nodded.

"So now what?" said Herson, looking at Chynoweth and Breuther, as were the others.

"They only told me to tell you that the boat is here and also that Chynoweth's father is here," said Breuther.

"So you don't know which one of us it is either," Jaka said to Breuther.

He shook his head.

"What if none of us go?" asked Jaka.

"But I want to go home from this place!" said one of the others.

"What if it's you?" asked another.

"It's not," he said.

"How do you know?"

"I just know."

"Breuther, they all should go," said one of the people already living inside the wall. Many had come closer and listened while Chynoweth and the children were talking.

"They should go, all of them. Now!"

"Or send them one at a time until the wanted child is found."

"And then the rest of them should go!"

"We will never send someone out of here," said Breuther. "You know that. You all know that."

"Do you think men with engines like that are just going to leave? They'll come in here to find what they want. And do you think, when they see all of us, all of this that you and your people have made to give to all of us, such men will just leave and never come back?" said one of the islandborn.

Breuther bit his lip.

He closed his eyes. He looked like a giant bearded child trying to remember his numbers.

"We. Will. Never. Send. Someone. Out. Of. Here."

"They should leave!"

"I want to go to the boat!"

"We should all go!"

"Sabel! Sabel!" said Theri, slapping Herson's hand from hers and pulling on her sleeve.

"What is it?" asked Sabel.

"It can't be one of us!" Theri said brightly.

"Why not?"

"How could Amma and Appa only want one of us? It has to be one of the only children. Sabel, if you have brother and sister, you're safe!"

Sabel looked at her. Theri was delighted. Sabel smiled and as quickly and imperceptibly as she could, she nodded. But she wasn't quick or imperceptible enough. While all the other children were rivalling their views back and forth and at Chynoweth, and the islandborn people were pointing at the door in the wall and saying angry things at silent Breuther, Reya and Verlane and S'Jin were close by and listening to Theri and Sabel, as were Jaka and Perdite and Gem. They were not exactly delighting, but they understood.

If you had brothers and sisters, you were safe.

"STOP! STOP IT! Stopitstopitstopitstopitstopit! It's me. It's always me," screamed jumping girl.

She walked to the door in the wall and didn't even turn to say goodbye to Sabel and her sisters before stepping through. Sabel wondered if she had already turned her attention to the next place she'd be sent to, the next place from where she'd have to figure out escape routes on the first day.

Meanwhile, everyone else became quiet.

They were listening for the engines to start.

Nothing.

After a few minutes, jumping girl stepped back through the door in the wall and returned to the group.

"It's not me," she said. For the first time, her voice wasn't metallic and flat. Instead it was metallic and surprised.

She pointed . . .

"It's you."

"You dummy! How can it be Jaka?" said Perdite.

"Dummy! DUMMY! They're not taking brothers from sisters! They're taking an only child. LIKE YOU, dummy! Jaka, tell her she's a dummy! Jaka! Tell her it's not you," said Gem.

"They said it's me?" asked Jaka.

Jumping girl nodded.

"Who said this?" he asked.

"Skinny man in sunglasses. Black skinny man in black sunglasses."

"PAPO! It's Papo! He's found us! He's found us and come to take us before Big Papo finds us!" said Jaka.

Beaming, triumphant, he began strutting around telling the cold, indifferent air and everyone sharing it that he had told them so, he had told them that his father would come for them before anyone else could, because he was a powerful man in trouble who was going to win in the end.

And this was the end.

"Papo must have found out Big Papo was coming for us, and got here first," Jaka said.

Perdite and Gem were biting on their fingers.

"Maybe it's Big Papo coming for us," Perdite said.

Jaka shook his head. "He's come for all three of us, my sweet dummies! He probably just said one child to get best price. Come on, let's all go see Papo."

"Jaka, can I come meet your Papo?" asked Tric.

"Everybody, come on! It's our Papo! We are safe! He is not going to let anything happen to us by those men," said Jaka. "You should come now, really, and get on the bus to go down to the boat while he is here. He will protect us until we get there. He has come here to protect us. Come!"

Jaka ran for the door in the wall, Tric and Gem and Perdite following. The rest of the children and Chynoweth went too.

Breuther was behind them. He was walking slowly because he was glaring at the islandborn people still on the inside. He would not forget his vow. But how could he forget what some of them had said just now? That all the children should be sent toward danger so that they could stay safe in their little sanctuary?

Jaka went first through the door. He looked around. The town square was full of bullet-headed young men who all looked like Gyre and Sidian. The bus was behind them, and jeeps were parked here and there. Was this a trick? Jaka turned to stop the rest of them from coming, but then he saw the looks on his sisters' faces.

"PAPO!"

Gem and Perdite ran to a tall thin man as he climbed out from one of the jeeps. He was wearing a ragged tan suit and tan army boots, shiny sunglasses and a broken smile.

He hugged the girls, and then he hugged Jaka, much much harder.

Everyone else watched them and felt happy for them and ached all the more for their own parents, including Chynoweth, who was looking for her father.

Meanwhile, Papo bent down and put his hands on the girls' shoulders and spoke to them. He then pointed to the side and told them to go.

The girls stepped back, stunned. Not even crying. Not even angry.

"He really is choosing Jaka over them," Reya said, standing against the wall with everyone else and immediately making plans to bring Gem and Perdite home with them instead.

Gem and Perdite stood their ground.

Papo motioned again for them to go.

Slowly, now sucking and heaving air into their birdcage ribcages and sobbing, the sisters suddenly looked like old women, widowed and childless. But only one of them would be, and not for many years. Bent and wracking, they moved only a little way away, then stopped and watched their father and brother.

Jaka pointed at Papo and said something hot and harsh and tried to bring back his sisters. Papo grabbed him and pulled him in close but said nothing. He only shook his head as he began speaking. Then it was Jaka who said nothing and only shook his head.

"Sam. Sam! It's time. Send him. Send the boy to me and we'll go."

The voice belonged to an older man. With an aide's help, he slowly climbed out of his own jeep. He was large and dark and wearing combat fatigues and heavy gold chains. He was smiling brightly. His mouth was full of metal and gold.

Big Papo.

Jaka, Gem and Perdite stared at their grandfather.

Then they stared at their father.

Their father stared at the ground.

Big Papo pointed at Jaka, held an open palm, waved it slightly, then turned his gloved hand and with his fat first finger, beckoned his grandson toward him.

Gem and Perdite tried to hold him back. Papo blocked them and hugged them so they wouldn't have to watch their brother walk away from them.

Jaka didn't turn around.

He walked to the rest of the life that was now his.

This was the deal. Jaka would go to Big Papo so that Gem and Perdite could go with Papo, who had defied Big Papo but whose life had now been spared.

Because Jaka had been traded to his grandfather, in exchange for his father and little sisters.

Big Papo made another motion with his hand and two of his men carried heavy-looking sacks to the bullet-headed young men and dropped them at their feet.

The noise in the silent square was like steel-handed applause, like a metal sky falling to earth, like heaps of gun and hard candy landing all at once.

Ghee. A lot of ghee.

The young men elbowed each other and writhed at their own mega futures.

"You were wrong about sisters and brothers," S'Jin spat at saucer-eyed Theri.

Verlane pushed him, and he jumped, wincing as he came down.

"Your ankle," said Tric matter of factly. "You're going to lose."

"What?" said S'Jin.

Tric sprinted into the square, past Gem and Perdite and Papo, and reached Jaka just as Jaka reached Big Papo.

"TRIC! Don't! Come back here!" Sabel called.

"He's not part of the trade," said S'Jin. "He'll be sent back."

Big Papo smiled and leaned in and listened as Tric whispered something to him. He nodded, and nodded, and nodded. Then he put a finger to the boy's mouth and asked a question.

Tric nodded and jumped up and down.

He wants to go with them! Sabel thought.

Jaka climbed into the jeep.

Tric followed.

But Big Papo pressed his hand into the boy's chest and pushed, pointing to a different jeep.

Tric turned and waved at the other children, who were calling him to come back. He tried to say something to Jaka, who was sitting in the back of Big Papo's jeep.

Jaka ignored him.

Looking very small and very alone, Tric went to the jeep directly behind. A black gloved hand pulled him in.

S'Jin sobbed. Theri held him close.

Papo took Gem and Perdite to his jeep.

One after the other, the jeeps behind the bus turned around in the little town square and drove away.

One of the men remaining there, in front of the bus, stepped to the side and Chynoweth's father appeared. Saying something over and over, he walked toward Chynoweth, who ran toward him. Behind their embrace, the cook appeared, followed by his wife and daughter. The cook had a bruised face.

Chynoweth led them to the door in the wall.

Breuther nodded and let them through.

After her father went inside, Chynoweth came back. She went back to the group of men and spoke with them, pointing at the other children and nodding.

"Children, it's time to get on the bus. It's time for you to go home. Jaka was right. His father will not leave the island until you are all on the boat that has come to take you back. It's time to get on the bus. It's time for us to say goodbye."

The boy with the mother in a workpartydress raised his hand. "I don't want to go back." He looked at Breuther, who nodded for him to walk through the door in the wall.

"Anyone else?" said Breuther.

"I don't want to go back either," said the girl who told everyone she came from the worst place of all. "I don't want to go back, but I will."

She walked to the bus. The other children followed.

Sabel squeezed Chynoweth's hand.

She was last to get onto the bus. From the window, she watched Chynoweth pass through the door in the wall. The door closed behind her.

Near the harbour were three empty jeeps. Two people were standing on a pier in front of the boat. Sabel could just see the shapes of two speedboats in the harbour. Big Papo and Jaka were on one, pulling away. Gem and Perdite were on the other, waiting.

The people on the pier were wearing high rubber boots and

storm jackets and sunglasses and masks and gloves, and holding clipboards.

They didn't say anything, waiting for the children to approach.

Daveedov went ahead and the rest followed, each giving a name before being sent onto the boat.

Sabel finally walked up the gangplank, seaspray hitting her on the shins.

Theson and Herson were the last ones.

Standing at a metal rail at the back of the ship, Sabel watched as the clipboard people checked, asked again, and shook their heads. They were shaking their heads at Herson.

They shook their heads again and turned and left.

Herson stood there, alone.

He's not going back home, Sabel thought. *His name isn't on the list to go back. Herson's mother hadn't sent for him.*

Herson looked up at Sabel and waved goodbye.

Sabel didn't wave back. She was gripping the rails and pretending they were gripping her so that she couldn't do anything but stand there and watch him, entirely alone on the pier of the island at the bottom and end of the fallen-down world.

Theri and Verlane hugged her at the waist.

Reya pressed her hands over Sabel's on the rail.

To let her know she was not alone.

"What do you mean he's not on the list?" screamed Theson, who'd run back to the clipboard people.

They didn't answer.

But suddenly Theson knew what it meant, just the same as Herson did. That Herson's mother didn't have enough ghee to pay for Herson to return, and Theson's mother wouldn't give her servant the ghee to get her boy back.

This meant that Theson would be going home by himself, to his mother and to the woman who had actually raised him alongside her own son, Herson.

The boss lady's son, Theson, would then have two mothers, and he would be totally alone.

Theson pushed past the clipboard people, down the gangplank and onto the pier.

One of the clipboard people said something and Theson waved them off. He went to Herson, who pointed at his chest and said something. He told him his name. Theson nodded and hugged him, and finally, they were acting like the brothers they had always been.

"OBA! OBA!"

The two of them looked up.

The OBA boys had been watching the whole time, from behind an abandoned cookshop. They were waiting there to see who would be left behind this time. They beckoned. Herson and Theson joined them. The boat left, and after a quiet meal, the children were jabbed again. They slept.

16

AND THIS IS WHAT SABEL and her siblings found, at the beginning of the rest of their lives:

Appa.

He was waiting for them in front of a new house in the dark blue light that comes well after night has passed but well before morning, in a part of the city they hadn't visited before or even knew existed.

He looked whole, like a crumpled paper flattened out.

They had a new house. It was a small house, one among many others. From the front walk it looked clean and empty.

"Appa! Appa, where's Amma? Why didn't she come outside to meet us?" asked Verlane.

He hugged them and brought them inside.

"Appa, where's Amma? Is she working at the hospital?" asked Theri.

He hugged them more and brought them to the kitchen, where a small morning meal was waiting.

"No. Where's Amma?" asked Reya.

"WHERE'S AMMA?" asked Sabel.

"They took her," he said finally.

"WHO?" asked S'Jin.

Appa shook his head.

"The new president. He needed doctors. He wanted the best."

"But you're a doctor too," said S'Jin. "Why didn't they take you? Aren't you the best?"

"She was so brave, children. She said she would go with them if they promised you would all be brought back. They said it was our only chance. So Amma said yes to the new president, and that's how we got the ghee to bring you back. And they gave us this house."

"She traded herself for us," said Sabel.

"We don't want this house," said Verlane. "We want Amma!"

"When is she coming back?" asked Theri.

"Why didn't they take you instead?" asked S'Jin.

Standing off to the side, answerless, Appa held his head in his hands. His shaking hands.

Amma always had the steady hands.

The children all noticed his shaking hands, except S'Jin, who was making plans to find his mother. He knew from his ten days away that unless he could find Jaka in his new mega-man life, he couldn't find her and bring her back from the falling-down world by himself. But unlike his father, he could try.

"I will get Amma back," S'Jin declared.

Sabel saw the look on S'Jin's face. They were all devastated and defeated, save S'Jin, who was devastated and determined.

Sabel decided she must be even more determined than he was.

She wondered how many times she would have to stomp on his ankle to stop him from going in search of Amma. But also, she wondered which would happen first: he would give up or she would give in.

She didn't wonder, actually. She knew she would give in first. Because from a deep, wrong-feeling, true place inside, she wanted him to grow up fast and go find Amma and bring her home. She did not believe he could. She only hoped Amma would come back before S'Jin went out into the falling-down world to find her.

And so, while she could, Sabel took charge.

She told everyone to sit for breakfast.

Clay cups of sour yoghurt.

No sweet syrup.

They prayed.

The children let go of each other and stared at their hands.

Randy Boyagoda is a novelist and professor of English at the University of Toronto. His novels, which include *Original Prin* and *Dante's Indiana*, have been nominated for the ScotiaBank Giller Prize and the IMPAC Dublin Literary Award. He lives in Toronto with his wife and four daughters. *Little Sanctuary* is his first novel for young readers.

The publisher thanks Karim Alrawi for his editorial advice.

Published in Canada in 2024. Published in the US and the UK in 2025 by Tradewind Books.

A portion of this novel appeared originally in *The Walrus* magazine, as "Little Sanctuary."

LIBRARY AND ARCHIVES CANADA CATALOGUING IN PUBLICATION

Title: Little sanctuary / Randy Boyagoda.
Names: Boyagoda, Randy, 1976- author.
Identifiers: Canadiana (print) 20240340051 | Canadiana (ebook) 20240340086 | ISBN 9781990598203 (hardcover) | ISBN 9781990598357 (softcover) | ISBN 9781990598210 (EPUB)
Subjects: LCGFT: Novels.
Classification: LCC PS8603.O9768 L58 2024 | DDC jC813/.6—dc23

Book design by Elisa Gutiérrez

The text is set in Garamond Premier. The book title is set in Tripper Rough Pro.

10 9 8 7 6 5 4 3 2 1

Printed and bound in Canada. The paper in this book came from Forest Stewardship Certified and Sustainable Forestry Initiative fibers.

FSC www.fsc.org MIX Paper | Supporting responsible forestry FSC® C016245

The publisher thanks the Government of Canada, the Canada Council for the Arts and Livres Canada Books for their financial support. We also thank the Government of the Province of British Columbia for the financial support we have received through the Book Publishing Tax Credit program and the British Columbia Arts Council.

British Columbia Arts Council | British Columbia

Supported by the Province of British Columbia

Canada Council for the Arts | Conseil des Arts du Canada | Canada